PENNY
for Your
THOUGHTS

Isabel
and Don

Hope you enjoy Penny's
life journey with her friends
on the Canadian prairies.

Rosemary 6-28-2019

(aka Shirley - a prairie
girl like you Isabel)

PENNY
for Your
THOUGHTS

Rosemary Vaughn

Mill City Press

Mill City Press, Inc.
2301 Lucien Way #415
Maitland, FL 32751
407.339.4217
www.millcitypress.net

Printed in the United States of America

ISBN-13: 978-1-54565-784-3

Dedicated to the memory of my parents,
Eldon and Rose Freeman,
whose stories about "the olden days"
of the Depression and World War II
I loved to hear.

To The Reader

Readers of *Love on the Misty Isles* will remember that toward the end of the novel, Sheryl, Libby, and her brother, Corbin, discovered that they had all come from the fictional Canadian prairie town of Crocus Plains, although Libby and Corbin had never known Sheryl when they lived there. This novel takes readers back to Crocus Plains with the introduction of a new main character, Penny Ryan. She and Sheryl grew up together, and Penny also knew Libby and Corbin when they came to town; therefore, this sequel also becomes a prequel. It is also somewhat of a family saga beginning with Penny's father Will's story. The time frame of the novel covers several decades from the 1930s to the first decade in the twenty-first century.

Since the crocus is the provincial flower of Manitoba, Crocus Plains is a fictional prairie town that represents all small towns in Manitoba. Elements of this fictional town may resemble some parts of the small town in which I grew up, Killarney, Manitoba. These elements have also been fictionalized. Readers who grew up on the prairies will relate to some of the places and activities that were common during various time periods represented in the novel.

In honour of my Canadian background, in this novel, I have used my birth nation's spelling of words that I remember from my youth. I had chosen not to do that in my debut novel.

It was at the urging of my readers who enjoyed my debut, award-winning novel, *Love on the Misty Isles*, that inspired me to write this sequel/prequel. So it is to you, my readers, that I am giving Penny and her life story for your thoughts. Does the story return to the Misty Isles? Read on to find out.

Rosemary Vaughn
2018
www.rosemaryvaughn.com

PROLOGUE

Stooping down with head bowed, the elderly gentleman gazed at the granite headstone. A light breeze wafted his thin grey hair as his body hunched over to see better. A tear squeezed between his squinting eyelids and trickled down his cheek.

Oak, maple, and ash trees surrounded the perimeter of the cemetery. It was early June, and the newly blossomed foliage danced in the light spring breeze. Penny pulled her sweater a little more tightly around her shoulders while watching her frail father focus on the headstone as he dealt with his surfacing emotions.

He had begged her to come to the personal care home where he resided in Brandon and bring him to Crocus Plains to visit the cemetery. After her mother had passed away a couple of years ago from lung cancer, Penny knew that her ailing father could not remain in her parents' home alone. The demanding responsibilities of her position as principal of the local high school prevented her from personally providing the care her father needed. The senior center in Crocus Plains was full, so she'd had him placed at one in the larger city of Brandon. It was a reputable home, and an easy hour-long drive to visit him on weekends or to make a quick trip if the need arose.

She had assumed that his request to come to the cemetery in his hometown had been for the purpose of visiting her mother's grave. Where they stood, however, was not in the part of the cemetery where her mother's grave existed, yet her father seemed visibly moved by whatever he was seeing and remembering.

Penny shifted slightly so that she could see the headstone more clearly. Her mouth fell open as she read the name engraved in the granite: "Grace (Harris) Ryan, 1920–1942, Beloved wife of William Thomas Ryan." This must have been her father's first wife.

What secrets and feelings had he harbored all these years? Well, she had a few secrets of her own.

CHAPTER ONE

*W*ill Ryan fidgeted in the wooden school desk. Fiddling with the strap buckles on his overalls, he glanced around the room to see if any of the other students were questioning who he was and why he was there. The other young fellows were dressed in freshly ironed khakis and colourful solid or striped shirts. They were obviously town kids. He knew he was older than these classmates, and he wondered if he would ever fit in.

He'd ridden his horse, Bonnie, to town. Several boys had snickered as they watched him tie her to the end of a bicycle rack near the base of the stairs leading up to the two-story stone building that housed the high school in the small prairie town of Crocus Plains, Manitoba.

Will had grown up on a grain farm west of town and had attended a country school that only went to grade nine. Thinking that he would probably spend his life on the family farm, Will hadn't thought about pursuing high school in town. When the dry dust bowl Depression years of the Dirty Thirties hit the prairies, however, Will realized that he shouldn't put all his eggs in one basket. Deciding to continue his education had brought him to today, sitting in a grade ten classroom at the age of seventeen.

Just as he was beginning to question his decision, an outburst of giggles drew his attention to the classroom door. In bounced two fifteen-year-old girls, arm in arm, heads together, whispering and laughing as they looked around the room for empty desks. One was tall and slender with shoulder-length honey-blond hair and sparkling blue eyes. She was dressed in a pastel blue and white gingham dress with a white Peter Pan collar, puffed sleeves, and a full skirt. Her friend was shorter and rounder with naturally curly brown hair, brown eyes, and a grin that radiated mischief. It was the radiation from the sparkling blue eyes, however, that drew Will's attention.

"Please find a seat, girls. We are about to start class," commanded the teacher, Miss McGrath. She was young and pretty but had an authoritative bearing that would tolerate no nonsense. The girls quickly found seats in different parts of the room, the blond one sliding into the empty desk across from Will. She smiled at him and said, "Hi! I'm Grace. What's your name?"

Will looked at this beautiful young gal, thinking her name suited her perfectly, and responded sheepishly, "I'm Will Ryan." Any further conversation was curtailed by Miss McGrath's frown directed at them and her instructions to take out their math texts.

It was a warm September day, so at noon Will took his sack lunch outdoors to sit on the steps. He wanted to check on Bonnie and give her the apple he'd packed for her. Most of the other students stayed in the classroom, but as Will held the apple out to Bonnie and stroked her neck, he felt a presence behind him. Turning to see who it was, he looked into those sparkling blue eyes of Grace. Smiling at him, she asked, "Who's your friend? What's he doing at school?"

"Her name is Bonnie, and I rode her into town from our farm. Do you live in town? I don't think I've seen you before."

"My dad opened the bank in town last spring, so we haven't been here that long. You've maybe heard of him. Robert Harris. Harris is my last name."

"I did know there was a new banker in town. My dad maybe knows him," he said a little hesitantly, knowing his dad had been to the bank looking for a loan to keep things afloat during these tough years on the farm.

"Do you come to town often, like on the weekends?" Grace asked with hope in her eyes.

"Sometimes on a Saturday night we'll come in to a dance if there's not one at Pine Ridge, the country school near our farm. My mum likes to come in on Sundays to church whenever we can."

"Oh, good. Maybe I'll see you sometime." The bell rang then to end the lunch hour.

After school, Grace stood on the school steps and waved to Will as he hoisted himself onto Bonnie and rode bareback down the main street and out of town.

* * *

That Saturday evening Will did come to town with his buddy Edward Stevens who lived on a farm half a mile from the Ryan farm. Edward had his parents' Model A, so the boys felt like they had hit the big time.

"Why were you so anxious to come to town tonight, Will?" Edward asked as he pulled up in front of the Town Hall where folks were gathering for the typical Saturday night dance.

"Well, Ed," Will hesitated, wondering how he should answer. "Thought we could have a little break from stooking hay."

"Hmmm. Okay," replied Ed, not quite believing this was the whole story.

As they entered the hall, they could hear the Walker family band trying to imitate the big band jazz sounds of the Swing Era. Standing just inside the door, Will caught sight of Grace across the room. At the same moment, she turned away from the two girls she was talking to and saw him. Hustling her two friends with her, she crossed the room, with a big smile on her face. When she reached the boys, she looked up at Will and exclaimed enthusiastically, "You came!"

Raising his eyebrows, Ed turned to Will with a look that said, *So this is the real reason we are here.*

"Hi, Grace. This is my friend Ed Stevens. Ed, this is Grace Harris. I met her at school. Her dad has the bank in town."

"Pleased to meet you, Ed," said Grace. Turning to the curly headed cutie Will recognized as Grace's friend from school, she continued, "This is my friend Nora Jensen and her little sister, Alma."

At that moment, the band struck up a polka. Grace and Nora reached out their hands toward the boys and said at once, as if rehearsed, "Shall we give it a try?" The two couples whirled and laughed as they spun in circles to the fast-paced tune, while Alma joined a group of girls her own age in the corner. When the polka ended, the band slowed the tempo to an old-time waltz. Will drew Grace into his arms, and she snuggled in as they danced cheek to cheek. Glancing over to his friend, Will noted that Ed and Nora were similarly engaged.

Thus began the courtships of the four young people. Will's mother was surprised when he insisted that they start going to church every Sunday in town. After church, while his mother visited with friends, Will and Grace would take a walk down to the lake. Along the way, they would stop in at the little lakeside confectionary store, and Grace, who always had extra coins in her pocket, would buy them a small bag of penny candy. His masculinity somewhat humiliated, one Sunday Will said the treat was on him, and he fished the nickel he'd kept from the collection plate out of his pocket to give to the storekeeper.

These Sunday walks were curtailed over the harsh winter months, but soon it was spring and they resumed. Sometimes

Will and Grace would sneak out of school at lunch and walk to the lake to spend some time alone. On one of these occasions, Will had told Grace he needed to talk to her. As they stood at the bridge dividing the bay from the lake, Grace looked up into Will's eyes and asked what he wanted to tell or ask her, hoping it was the latter.

Before answering, Will slid his arms around her waist and bent his head to kiss her tenderly and deeply. She responded in kind. Pulling away, Will finally explained, "I can't continue school, Grace. My family is finding it hard to make a go of it on the farm in this depression. We always have lots to eat because Mum plants a great garden and has learned to stretch dishes with cream sauce, but we need seed for the crops, and the machinery is wearing out and is too expensive to replace. That's only part of it, but I'm going to have to find a job to help out and save some money if we're ever going to be able to get married."

"Oh, Will! I'd marry you tomorrow!" Grace exclaimed.

"No, Grace. We have to be sensible. You need to finish school. Your parents would be upset if you quit and got married so young. We can wait." Will had always felt her parents were a little skeptical about their daughter's relationship with this farm boy.

"Okay," Grace agreed reluctantly, "but promise me this isn't the end of us."

"Of course it's not," Will stated, drawing her in again for a passionate kiss.

CHAPTER
TWO

*W*ill went to work for his Uncle George, his dad's brother, at the Case dealership that George had opened after giving up on farming during these rough times. Will had always been handy working on any mechanical problems they'd had with the family's farm machinery, so he was an asset to his uncle. As well as trying to make a better living for his family, George also wanted to help his farming friends and neighbours get the best deals in service and the purchase of new or used equipment.

After three years, Will's expertise in machinery and his easy-going manner made him a popular salesman in Uncle George's business. He finally felt economically secure enough to marry Grace, who had graduated from high school and worked part time in the Higgins House Ice Cream Parlour.

On a warm, sunny day in June, Will and Grace and Ed and Nora took their vows in the large, beautifully landscaped back-yard of Grace's parents' home. The banker hadn't suffered quite as much as other people during the Depression. The service was performed by the new United Church minister, who was awaiting the building of the new church. In 1925, the Presbyterians, Methodists, and Congregationalists of Canada had joined to form this new Protestant sect, and Crocus Plains was awaiting the remodel of their old Methodist church to serve its new, larger congregation.

The young people served as witnesses for each other's nuptials. Ed had gone to work for the grain elevator agent, and he and Nora were moving into the apartment above the hardware store. Grace's folks had provided the young Ryans with a small house across the tracks from the elevator that they normally rented to others.

* * *

A year later, Will swung boyishly as he walked down the street toward Mrs. Potter's house. It was a beautiful day, like the day he and Grace were married, and he was a happy man. He shouldn't have been; it was 1942, and his country was at war. But he couldn't help it. His Grace was having a baby. He was a young man and felt a little guilty for not having signed up for military service. He wanted to join his buddy Ed who'd signed up a couple of weeks ago, but he felt he should stay with Grace until the baby was born, after which she could move in with her folks and he would volunteer. It was his duty. But today, he was going to be a father.

With the sun reflecting off his sandy hair, Will hummed the popular wartime song "Lili Marlene" as he strode confidently toward the little house at the end of the street, gravel crunching beneath his feet. He paused a moment at the gate of the little picket fence, then swung it open, walked down the hollyhock-lined path, and leaped lightly onto the porch, taking two steps at a time. He spotted hot pink and white variegated bachelor's buttons in the window box. Their ragged edges made them look like tiny carnations. Grace loved carnations. These would have to do.

There was no hospital in the little Canadian town of Crocus Plains, so Grace was "lying -in" at Mrs. Potter's house, as most of the expectant mothers did when their time came. Mrs. Potter was a midwife from the old country, as the townsfolk referred to any place in Europe or the British Isles. She helped a lot of babies arrive into the world. She was a big help to ol' Doc Adams, who travelled the countryside in his dilapidated Model T. Doc couldn't be everywhere, but God knows he tried. The people of the area knew they were lucky to have him, and they overlooked his tendency to tip the bottle a little.

Will had just come from Doc's home, where he'd left the message with Doc's wife that it was Grace's time and she was at Mrs. Potter's. Doc was down in Hungry Hollow checking on the O'Kelly children, who had the measles. Paddy O'Kelly never seemed to be able to quite make a living out of his little farm down by the river, and that's why the townsfolk had dubbed his place Hungry Hollow. Doc would be lucky to get a scrawny chicken for his trouble, but that wouldn't bother Doc. Will hoped Doc would get back soon, but there was plenty of time. He remembered that first babies weren't in a hurry to be born.

Will arranged the bachelor's buttons into a small bouquet and tapped on the front door. There was no answer. Realizing Mrs. Potter was probably with Grace, Will opened the door and stepped inside. It was peaceful . . . no, it was quiet—too quiet. His palms suddenly felt clammy, and the back of his neck prickled with dampness. He forced himself down the hallway and bounded up the stairs, not lightly this time, but with an urgency borne of fear.

He burst through the bedroom door into the room where Grace lay. The shades were drawn. Bent over Grace's lower body, Mrs. Potter turned fear-stricken eyes toward him. "Did you find Doc Adams?" she demanded.

"What's wrong?" He knew something was terribly wrong. Then he saw the blood. Everywhere.

"Did you get Doc?" Mrs. Potter's voice rose frantically as she grabbed another towel in her futile attempt to stop the bleeding.

Will was dazed. "No . . . no. He's at the O'Kellys," he stammered. He made himself move his heavy legs toward the head of the bed then knelt beside it. Grace's eyes were closed, her face was a ghastly white, and her blond hair lay limp against the pillow. Will leaned over her. Her breath barely brushed his cheek.

"She began hemorrhaging about half an hour ago." Mrs. Potter's forehead and upper lip glistened with sweat. "Poor wee thing's lost a lot of blood. Too much."

Will tucked the bouquet into Grace's hand, curling her limp fingers around the stems. He brushed the hair away from her eyes, which flickered open. Her feverish blue eyes pleaded with him, then closed.

* * *

Mrs. Potter and Doc Adams stood at the lace-curtained parlour window and watched the broken young man walk, head bent, past the hollyhocks to the gravel road.

"To lose them both. It's too much," Mrs. Potter moaned. "If only I'd. . . ."

"Don't blame yourself. You couldn't have done anything, Marjorie." Doc turned sad, bloodshot eyes toward her. "I couldn't have done anything either. The placenta separated from the lining too soon. Without that, the wee one had no oxygen, and Grace lost too much blood." He sighed, exasperated. "It's times like these I hate being a country doctor. I hate not having a hospital and specialists. I feel so . . . helpless."

"Don't be so hard on yourself, Doc." Marjorie patted his shoulder. They turned again toward the window and watched Will make his way down the gravel road. The setting sun no longer brought a luster to his bent blond head.

CHAPTER
THREE

$\mathcal{A}$ few days after the simple funeral service in the United Church and the burial in the cemetery, Will stood before the cement headstone that bore his wife's name, Grace Ryan, 1920–1942. It would be several years later that Grace's family would replace the rough-hewn, simple headstone with a granite one that emphasized her maiden name, Harris.

Will still couldn't believe what had happened. How could he have lost his soul mate and baby boy at the same time? Yes, it had been a baby boy. Tears started to sting his eyes, so he bowed his head, and holding his forehead in his hand, he let the tears flow. His shoulders shook with emotion.

After a few minutes, he felt someone sidle up to him and a small hand begin to rub his back. He lifted his head a bit and, looking down, he saw that it was Nora, Ed's wife and Grace's best friend. She was sobbing just as hard as he was.

"I'm so sorry, Will. I don't know what to say. There's nothing I can say to ease your pain. To ease my own." Nora reached up to put her arms around his neck, bringing his head down in line with her cheeks and holding him close. "You can't be alone right now, and neither can I. Come for supper and we can talk about Grace, the baby, and Ed. I'm so afraid I'm going to lose him, too."

Ed had volunteered just a couple of weeks ago with the Winnipeg Rifles, nicknamed the "Little Black Devils" by earlier enemies. He would be leaving today for Peterborough, Ontario, for quick basic training before being shipped to the European front in the war. World War I was supposed to be the war to end all wars, but here they were again, fighting a brutal dictator in Germany to end the destruction he was causing in Europe.

At supper, Will confessed that he couldn't stay here in Crocus Plains, where he would have to confront his loss every day. "I think I'm going to sign up tomorrow. Maybe I'll catch up to Ed and we can face the enemy together." Nora stood up from her chair and put her arms around his neck, hugging his head to her chest, tears glistening in her eyes.

Because of the controversy over conscription in World War I, there was no overseas conscription yet. At their ages, Will and Ed weren't required to sign up, but they both had felt it their duty to volunteer. In World War I, Canada's ties to Britain were still so strong that when England had declared war, Canada was also automatically at war. There had been some dissent about conscription during that war, especially among the Quebec French Canadians. This time around, even though Canada was still a part of the Commonwealth, it had been working on its autonomy. Therefore, when Britain declared war against Germany this time, it was a week later and after Parliament had voted on the issue that Canada also declared war.

As he had told Nora, the next day Will left for Winnipeg and signed up with the Winnipeg Rifles. The day following, he and other new recruits rode the train to Peterborough, Ontario. There Will was put through rigorous training. More troops were needed overseas, so the military needed to beef up the preparation of the infantry to get the new troops shipped out as soon as they could to help those already at the front.

In Peterborough, Will connected with his buddy Ed. Ed hadn't been in touch with Nora recently, so he was shocked and bereaved at the news of Will's loss. Within a few weeks, they boarded the Queen Mary, a former luxury liner that had been converted to carry troops during the war, and sailed to Britain.

CHAPTER
FOUR

Being prairie boys, Will and Ed found the trip across the Atlantic an exhilarating yet anxiety-producing adventure. Not knowing what to expect upon arrival in London added to their mixed feelings about embarking on this journey.

Will and Ed made an effort to become acquainted with other soldiers on the voyage who came from a variety of backgrounds and several different regions of Canada. Knowing that these fellows would be sharing their wartime experiences, they also came to realize they would become dependent on one another for their lives.

Finally arriving at the wharf in London, the troops disembarked and climbed into the trucks that would take them to their camps, where they joined one of the many Canadian Infantry Divisions. Driving through the streets of London, the new troops witnessed some of the destruction the German Luftwaffe had done to the city during the Battle of Britain. Part of the Canadian infantry's mission was to defend England and the UK, and the new troops began training for land attacks across the channel, where Germany had already overtaken Poland, France, and the Netherlands.

Ed and Will managed to stick together at their assigned stations and barracks. When they had leave from duties, they would go into London to grab a beer at a pub and visit with the locals and other soldiers and airmen. Canadian pilots were helping the RAF defend England from the German air strikes. Although they had tried different pubs, some of which had been around for centuries, Roberts Roost had become Will and Ed's favourite haunt. It was run by two brothers, John and Larry Roberts, whose father Joseph had begun the public ale house earlier in the twentieth century, just before the First World War. Joe still showed up once in a while to visit with his old buddies who'd been regulars ever since he'd opened the place. Ed and Will were soon on a first-name basis with the brothers.

One evening, a new barmaid approached Will and Ed's table, and looking directly at Will, noting his uniform, she grinned and asked, "Hey, Canada, what's your pleasure tonight?"

Startled, Will looked up into warm brown eyes while the guys at the next table started razzing him. "Yeah, Will, what's your pleasure tonight?" one said. Another replied, "I'm sure she'll accommodate."

Overhearing these comments, the brothers came out from behind the bar and moved toward the tables. Before they arrived, Will turned to the other table and said, "Knock it off, Yanks. That's no way to treat a lady." Embarrassed, his fellow soldiers from the United States, who had recently joined the European front in the UK, immediately backed off, apologizing for offending her and explaining that they had only meant to tease Will.

When the brothers reached the table, John said, "Thanks, Will, for coming to our sister's defense. This is Maude, our little sister. She's been volunteering with the Red Cross, but she's decided to help us out in the evenings."

"So, what can I get for you fellows tonight?" Maude asked. Will began apologizing again for his fellow soldiers. She laughed, saying, "Hey, no problem. I'm a big girl. I know how to handle jerks. After all, I grew up with two brothers."

Chuckling at her, Larry said, "I'll get these guys their usual on the house. You can bring it to them."

Over the next few months, Will and Ed visited with Maude and learned that one of the reasons she had started working evenings for her brothers was that they were thinking of helping their country by joining up. The Royal Air Force had had some success against the Luftwaffe, so recruiting posters had begun sporting the quote from Prime Minister Churchill's radio broadcast recognizing the RAF's contribution to the war effort: "Never was so much owed by so many to so few." As it had others, this phrase inspired the Roberts boys to do their part. Maude, therefore, wanted to learn the pub business to help her father in case someday they had to take over the place for her brothers.

One slow evening, she joined Will and Ed at their table. During their conversation, Ed pulled a piece of stationery from his pocket and said, "I got a letter from Nora today. She sent it a couple of months ago, but you know how our mail gets delayed. Anyway, she has some news." He hesitated.

"Well, what is it?" Will asked. "Spill the beans."

Still a little cautious, Ed read, *So, sweetheart, I guess our big night before you left had its rewards. Yes, I'm pregnant. Wish you were here to share the joy, but since you're not, do you have any suggestions for names? I'm thinking if it's a boy, he should be Edward after you. We can call him Eddie.*

Looking at Will with sad eyes, he added, "I know this must be hard on you, Will. Nora does, too, and she sends her love."

Maude, looking at Will quizzically, said, "Congratulations, Ed. It must be hard for you to be so far away."

"Yes, Ed. Congratulations," Will concurred. "Don't worry about me. Just make sure you tell Nora to take care of herself and your little one, and to get the best care possible."

Ed immediately started writing a response to Nora. In it he tells her that because it might be too confusing to have two Eds in the family, he would like to name a son after Will. *We could name him William Edward after both of us and call him Billy for short. If it's a girl, I hope she's as cute and fun as her mother. Your choice for a name.*

Still looking at Will with her eyebrows pulled together, Maude stated, "Well, I'm off for the night, guys. Take care."

"I'll walk you home," Will said, pushing back his chair. "Young women shouldn't be out this late on their own. One never knows what will happen next these days."

During their walk, Will explained to Maude that he had been married and what had happened to his wife and unborn son. Maude's eyes filled with tears, and when they reached her doorstep, she hugged him and kissed him on the cheek. "You are such a wonderful man. I can't imagine what you've been through. I will always be here for you if you need to talk. It's the least I can do. You've been so helpful to us in bringing food and other things we can't get because of the rationing. My brothers think you and Ed are just the best. They think of you as a brother."

Walking Maude home became a habit whenever Will was able to take a break and come to the city's pub center.

CHAPTER
FIVE

 *F*rance and the Netherlands surrendered to Germany after the Germans started a Blitzkrieg (lightning war) against these countries. Inspired by Churchill's quote, John and Larry Roberts did enlist.

When Hitler recognized the efforts and successes of the RAF during the Battle of Britain and the "never give up" stamina of the English people, he vowed to destroy London and other major cities in the country. Germany upscaled its air attacks on England with daytime bombing by the Luftwaffe, destroying parts of the cities, and eventually added Blitzkrieg attacks in the night. Although most of the Blitz had ended in 1941, intermittent air raids continued throughout the war. Blackouts to camouflage the English cities' locations and warning sirens of attack planes had become commonplace and continued beyond the Battle of Britain.

Will was at Roberts Roost alone one evening while Ed was writing a letter to Nora during his break while on duty at their camp. Maude had just brought Will his usual mug of ale when the Blitzkrieg warning sirens began screaming. While her father, Joe, herded the few customers out of the pub, Maude grabbed Will's hand and, pulling him from his chair, shouted, "We have to get to shelter!" They ran down the street and into the underground railroad tunnel. Beginning as an impromptu shelter, the Tube had been officially designated as a shelter during bombing attacks.

Mothers comforted crying children while fathers circled their families in their arms. Looking down at Maude, Will saw the anxiety in her eyes and felt the nervous trembling of her hand still within his. He squeezed it, encircled her shoulders with his other arm, and pulled her to him. "It's okay, Maudie. I'm here. I know you're worried about your brothers, and about us here right now, but we have strong troops within our allies, and we have to have faith that we will come through this."

Maude raised her eyes, which were brimming with tears, to him and asked, "Did you call me Maudie?"

"Yes," Will replied. "Guess I feel we've become close enough that Maudie seems more intimate." With that he leaned down and kissed her for the first time full on the mouth with a passion that expressed more than friendship.

Maude responded fully, and when they pulled apart, she asked another question. "Does this mean you feel about me the same as I feel about you?"

"I guess it does." Will smiled down at her just as the "all clear" sounded.

Their love and relationship continued to grow during the infrequent times they were able to spend time together.

* * *

Canadian, British, and US infantries had been preparing for a combined raid on Dieppe, a French coastal port, to shake up the enemy. The Canadian troops took the lead in this invasion, with several thousand men involved. The Brits contributed a thousand troops, and the recently involved US provided a handful of Rangers. Unfortunately, the Germans learned of the planned raid and were waiting on the cliffs on each side of Dieppe and fired at the oncoming troops. The end was a disaster, with thousands of Canadians killed, wounded, or captured. The British and Americans suffered some losses as well.

Maude sat in Roberts Roost, with her elbows leaning on a table and her hands supporting her head as she sobbed. Her brothers Larry and John stood on each side of her, patting her back. They had just returned from the raid unharmed, but being in a different unit than Will, they didn't know of his situation. The rumor was that over half of the Canadian soldiers would not be returning to England, having either been killed, severely wounded, or taken prisoner.

The door to the pub swung open and a disheveled Canadian soldier walked toward the table. "Maudie, I'm here," he said as he reached the threesome. Stunned, the brothers backed away, and Maude looked up into the bruised face of her beloved Will.

Jumping up into his arms, Maude cried out, "Thank God, thank God! You're safe!" Then, gently touching his cheek, she kissed him deeply. "I couldn't have lived without you," she whimpered, breaking into tears again.

"Don't ever say that, my Maudie. You are strong, and life must always go on. But I'm here, and I plan to stay."

"Of course, Will," she replied, remembering the tragic losses he had survived in his life. Larry and John slapped Will's back in celebration of their buddy's survival and return.

At that moment, the door opened again, and in strode Ed, holding a letter in his hand. "Hi, guys. I don't know what route Nora's letter took, but it was waiting for me when I stopped out at our camp. I'm a father! Nora has blessed me with a baby boy, William Edward Stevens. Here's a picture of my wee Billy."

More slapping of backs occurred as the guys congratulated Ed, and Maude kissed the picture of baby Billy, and then his dad.

* * *

After a year of continuing to help defend the UK and prepping for other operations, Ed became a part of a combined forces unit to invade mainland Europe through Italy. He and Will would be separated until their units met later in the Netherlands.

Meanwhile, Will and Maude had several months together before Will became a part of the raid on Normandy. The failure at Dieppe had taught the operations how to improve on preparation for this next major invasion, and it was a success.

Upon his return from Normandy, Will told Maude they needed to talk. She looked at him with concern, wondering if this was the end of their relationship.

"Why do you look worried, Maudie? Don't you think you'd like Canada?"

"What?" Maude asked. "What are you talking about?"

Grinning, Will chuckled. "Oh, guess I jumped over some of the details. I love you, Maudie, and I want you to be my wife. When this hell we're living in is over, I want us to make our home together in Canada."

"Will, really? Of course. I want nothing more than to be with you, no matter where we live."

"Are you sure you're okay with leaving your dad and your brothers? I'll ask their permission, of course."

"I'm an adult, Will. I can make my own decisions, but I know they'll be fine with it. They love you almost as much as I do. A little differently, I guess," she giggled. "I just wish my mother were here to share this happiness with me. What about your family? Will they approve of me?"

"They'll adore you and will be so thankful that you and your family have been here for me during these trying times. After I've talked to your father and brothers, I'll talk to my commanding officer. After realizing love matches during wartime are inevitable, the Army has become much more helpful in assisting in the arrangement of marriages."

Although they would miss her when she'd leave London, her father, Joe, and her brothers, John and Larry, gave their blessing and hosted their small, casual ceremony, performed by the pastor from Will's infantry, and the following reception with a few friends at Roberts Roost. Will's only regret was that Ed was not there to be his best man and witness their marriage.

The young couple was about to go to Maudie's suite to make the love they'd been yearning for when a soldier rushed into the pub with orders for Will to report back to their station. Their units were about to embark on a campaign to liberate the Netherlands.

With much regret over not consummating their marriage, Will and Maudie hugged and kissed passionately. Will promised emphatically, "I will return."

Maudie responded just as firmly, "And I will be here."

Liberating the Netherlands was the culmination of the Canadian contribution to the war. The people of the area were forever grateful for this liberation, as well as for the relief from starvation and sickness the Canadians brought to them. Today, their efforts are still honoured overseas, especially in Holland.

Ed and Will reconnected after Ed's unit worked its way through Italy to the Netherlands. There the two groups made a joint Canadian Corps in liberating the Netherlands. Other units had gone on to assist in the Western Allied invasion of Germany.

After the liberation operation, Ed and Will returned to London. Will was anxious to see his bride, and Ed was happy for his buddy but was anxiously hopeful to be heading home soon. Indeed, shortly after they arrived back in London, Germany surrendered. Some of the soldiers, especially those who had come later into service, would be staying on for the occupation of Germany. Ed and Will were soon to be shipped back to Canada.

Together at last, Will and Maudie made love as if it was not only their first time, but as if it were their last. Unfortunately, it was going to be their last for a while. Will's unit was shipping out shortly. They made an appointment with the Canadian Wives' Bureau in London, which had been established to assist spouses and families of service men or women in joining their spouses in Canada.

"I'll make sure he behaves himself until you get there, Maude," Ed promised with a chuckle.

"Thanks, Ed." Maude grinned. "I can hardly wait to meet your Nora and wee Billy."

"Go get us a place on the ship, a-hole!" Will said to Ed with mock disgust.

"I can take a hint, buddy," Ed replied, laughing.

Drawing Maude into his arms, Will whispered in her ear, "I love you to the moon and back, and I won't be happy until we are together loving to the moon and back."

Maude responded with a passionate kiss that promised many more to come. After Will had climbed onboard, she tearfully waved to both guys, who waved back from the railing along the side of the ship.

CHAPTER
SIX

*T*he trip across the ocean was less stressful this time than the first trip. Will and Ed were going home aboard the Isle de France, another luxury liner repurposed to be a troop transporter. Instead of the anxiety of going to war, they experienced relief and excitement about reconnecting with their family, friends, and homeland. Will felt a little regret as he'd left his love behind, but with luck, she would be joining him soon in Canada.

The ship wound its way down the St. Lawrence River into Lake Ontario and docked in Toronto. The troops disembarked and searched out their varying ways home. Will and Ed found their way to the train station and got tickets on a Canadian Pacific Railway train to Manitoba. Ed had written Nora about their expected date of arrival in Winnipeg, telling her they would catch a ride with some other soldiers from the Crocus Plains area.

As the train pulled into the station, Will was looking out the window at all the families waiting on the platform for their returning soldiers. Suddenly, he nudged Ed with his elbow and said, "Look, Ed, over there by that pillar. It looks like Nora and a little kid."

Ed immediately scoured the crowd for his wife and saw her with a little toddler. "That must be Billy!" he exclaimed. He and Will rushed to the door and were the first ones off the train, running toward Nora. When she saw them, she grabbed the toddler's hand and started running toward them, calling, "Come on, Billy, there's your daddy!"

Ed scooped Nora into his arms while Will shook Billy's hand and introduced himself as his daddy's friend. Ed finally let Nora go and scooped Billy into his arms while Nora hugged Will. "I'm so glad you got home safe and sound. I only wish Grace were here to greet you, too." Kissing him, she added, "This is from her."

"Thanks, Nora. I'm glad to be home, but I have some news to share. Of course I miss Grace and always will. She was my first love. But God sent me another angel to save me from my grief. I met her in London. Her name is Maude, and we were married before Ed and I were shipped home. I'm hoping that she won't be far behind."

Nora withdrew herself from him and, looking up at him, questioned, "Really?"

"I know Grace was your best friend, Nora, but I'm sure you'll like my Maudie, and I hope you'll help her adjust to her new home."

"I'll try. But right now we have something else to discuss. I've arranged to have Billy baptized this Sunday, and Ed and I would like you to be his godfather. After all, he's named after you."

Watching Ed cuddling and tickling his son, Will grinned and replied, "I'd be honored." He wondered if he'd ever have a son of his own.

Walking to the Stevenses' car, Will offered to drive so Ed could focus on his wife and little boy. Upon their arrival in Crocus Plains, Will and Ed were surprised to see a crowd of townsfolk on the main street gathered in front of the Town Hall. The high school band was playing "O Canada" under a banner stretched across the doorway that stated, "Welcome Home, Ed and Will, Our Heroes!"

After the mayor gave a short speech in honour of the men, Will responded, "Thank you for all this honour. We appreciate it, but we only did what any one of you would have done for our country and our friends and family. We are very glad to be back with you."

The people cheered and greeted the guys with hugs and handshakes as they made their way through the crowd and toward home.

Going to the little house across the track that Grace's parents had provided for them, Will began to wonder if it would be an appropriate home to bring his Maudie to. She might be uncomfortable being in his first wife's house, knowing that he would probably be haunted with sad memories. And what would the Harrises think of his bringing a new wife to the home they'd provided for him and their daughter? He'd have to give this situation some serious thought.

CHAPTER
SEVEN

*A*fter a couple of days of getting settled back into civilian life and visiting his parents on their farm, Will started back at his old job. Uncle George had saved his job for him at the Case dealership while Will had been serving their country. On his first day back, Will confided in his uncle the quandary he faced in bringing his new bride home to the house he had shared with Grace.

"I understand your dilemma, Will, and I might be able to help," said George, laying his hand sympathetically on Will's shoulder. "You remember the little white house up the lane from our shop here? Well, I bought it a few years ago, thinking one of our girls might settle back home here in Crocus Plains. But your cousins both got married while you were overseas, and their husbands are brothers from Morden, where they have important research jobs at the Experimental Farm. So Deb and Barb, being good dutiful wives, have made their homes with them in Morden. That leaves me with a little house that I'm going to have to sell. If you think it would work, I'd gladly sell it to you at a reasonable price. You can pay me back gradually over a long period of time. I know it's going to take time to get your feet back on the ground."

"Really, Uncle George? I can't thank you enough. And I'm sure the Harrises will be glad to be rid of me, too."

"After what you've done for our country, Will, it's the least I can do. And since we will be working together as partners, I think you better start calling me George."

Looking at George quizzically, Will asked, "What do you mean 'partners'? I'm your employee."

"At the moment, Will." George grinned. "Since my daughters won't be taking over my dealership, I plan to eventually make you a partner so I have someone I trust to take over the business when I'm too old to carry on. I've been feeling that may be sooner rather than later."

"Oh, don't say that Uncle . . . er, I mean, George. But I'd be honoured to be your partner. What opportunities you have presented to me. Too bad Deb and Barb are married. Maudie's brothers, Larry and John, would have been perfect matches for them, and we could have made it a family business. Anyway, with all you've given me, I'm feeling much more confident in what I have to offer my Maudie when she arrives in Canada."

"I hope that's soon, Will. I'm looking forward to meeting her. It will be quite a challenge for her to come to a new country and begin a whole new life."

"You'll love her," Will predicted. "And she's strong. She'll see this as an adventure more than a challenge. I'm hoping to hear that she's on her way in the next couple of weeks."

* * *

Indeed, a few days after this conversation, Will received a telegram from Larry saying she would be embarking on her journey across the Atlantic on the Queen Mary the following Friday. The Canadian Wives' Bureau had arranged her passage as well as train accommodations to Brandon, Manitoba. She would arrive two weeks from her departure date.

The expected date of arrival came, and Will stood on the platform at the Brandon train station, wringing his hands in hope that she would be on the train and that nothing unanticipated had prevented her arrival. Soon he heard the forlorn call of the train's whistle announcing its arrival and the chugging of the engine as it got closer. Watching it pull into the station and hearing the hiss and screech of the brakes as it slowed down, Will bowed his head, saying quietly to himself, "Please, God, let her be on it."

The porters placed the stepping stools outside the car doors, and the passengers began flowing off the train. There were still some soldiers just arriving home being greeted by their families. There were a few young women, probably also war brides, whisked into the waiting arms of their husbands or lovers.

Becoming impatient and anxious, Will wondered, *Where is my Maudie?* Shortly thereafter, he saw a porter a few cars down the track raise his hand to help a young woman down from the car's door onto the stool and then the platform. She was a small woman dressed neatly in a brown tweed suit with a coordinated tan beret. When she touched the ground, her brown eyes scanned the waiting crowd.

Will called out, "Maudie!" as he ran toward the petite woman. Seeing him, Maudie began running also, stumbling a bit in her pumps. Reaching him, she jumped into his outstretched arms. Crushing her to his chest, he whispered in her ear, "Thank God you are here. I've missed you so much!"

Pulling back slightly from him, she said, "Me too," then pressed her lips to his. The kissing turned more and more passionate as Will's hand slid down her back. He pulled her bottom closer to him, and her legs dangled from his grip, with the tips of her toes barely touching the platform. Hearing the "woohoo" sounds of the people around them, they pulled apart, cheeks flushing in embarrassment.

Will set Maude on the ground. "Better get you home, Mrs. Ryan. We have an hour's drive, and I'm not sure I can wait that long to truly welcome you to your new home."

Grinning up at him, she grabbed his hand and replied, "Agreed, Mr. Ryan. I've been waiting several weeks, so I can wait another hour, but let's get going."

They made their way to the Ford Deuce Coupe that he'd borrowed from his Uncle George. "Will all my stuff fit in the boot?" Maudie asked.

Frowning, Will looked at her and started to question, "What do you mean . . . oh, I remember. You mean the trunk." He grinned at her and said gently, "You'll have to do some adjusting to our Canadian English."

Maude nodded her head in agreement as they loaded her steamer trunk and suitcase. As she headed to the driver's side of the car, Will redirected her, and they both climbed into the car and headed to their first home.

On the hourlong drive to Crocus Plains, Maude described her uncomfortable trip across the ocean, saying she had often felt nauseated and that she had upchucked her breakfast at times.

"Oh, that's pretty natural," Will laughed. "Many of the boys going to and from war did the same."

"Yes," Maude hesitated. "Some of the other gals were in the same mess. There sure were some interesting women from all over the UK going to different places in Canada and the US. I had a really intriguing chinwag with a woman on the train who was going to Saskatchewan. She said her future husband had a huge prairie dog ranch out there. She's quite excited. Guess she's got a real winner!"

Will almost choked laughing at her and her new friend's naivety. Pulling himself together, he explained that prairie dogs were basically just wild gophers, often making little communities out of mounds on the prairies.

"Oh dear, you mean he lied to her?" Maude fussed. "I hope she's not disappointed and that things work out for them."

"If she truly loves him, it will probably be fine. And he probably didn't lie, he just exaggerated a little. I imagine the young soldier must have wanted to give her a feeling of security in leaving her home to follow him to this new country."

"But I would follow you anywhere, no matter what you had to offer. You didn't have to make any big false promises," Maude exclaimed.

Reaching over with his right hand to pat her knee, Will agreed. "I know, Maudie. We have true love, and I would never try to mislead you."

"I know, Will, but. . . ." She paused.

"But what?"

Looking at him with worry in her soft brown eyes, she continued, "Aren't you driving on the wrong side of the road?"

Patting her on her knee again and smiling at her gently, he relieved her anxiety by explaining another difference she would need to get used to in her new home. Understanding dawning on her, she acknowledged, "Oh, I get it. That's why the steering wheel is on that side and I had to sit over here. I'll try really hard to learn so I can fit in and not embarrass you."

"You could never embarrass me, and I love you just the way you are. I just want you to feel comfortable here so you'll have no regrets leaving your country and your family. I'll always be here for you, Maudie."

"And me for you," she confirmed, smiling with adoration in those soft brown eyes.

Reaching the southern central area of Manitoba, they soon entered the town of Crocus Plains, and Maude eagerly absorbed as much as she could. Will explained that the main street was called Central Avenue and that it went through the center of town, ranging from the grain elevators on the railroad tracks,

through the business section, past the schools and a few residences to Jackfish Lake at the opposite end of town. Turning
off Central Avenue midway through the business section, Will
pointed out his Uncle's dealership where he worked as they
passed it on their way up the back lane to the house Will had
purchased from his uncle. Pulling up to the small white lap-sided
house, Will declared, "Here we are. We're home." He unloaded
the trunk, and after placing her baggage inside the backdoor
entrance, he carried his bride over the threshold into the kitchen.

After Maudie used the only bathroom, which was just off
of the kitchen, Will gave her a quick tour of the two small bed-
rooms and the combined living room/dining room. He'd have to
explain later that the town had no public waterworks, so in the
summer they would use the outhouse in the garage and a porce-
lain chamber pot at night. This way they wouldn't overuse the
cistern water and septic tank that were installed for indoor water
and sanitary use in the frigid snowy winters. After the tour, they
settled at the table in the small kitchen to delve into the supper
Aunt Betty and Uncle George had left for the newlyweds.

Exhausted, they decided to retire early in the bedroom they'd
chosen at the front of the house, which faced the street. It had a
full-sized bed, which Aunt Betty had prepared with sheets, pil-
lows, and a beautiful quilt that she and Will's mother had made
for the young couple.

Her back to Will, Maude pulled off her suit, blouse, bra, and
slip. As she loosened the bobby pins from her victory roll, Will
came up behind her and slid his arms around her, hands sliding
up the front of her torso to her breasts. "Hmmm," he groaned.
"You couldn't have lost too much by throwing up on the ship.
I think you've filled out a little, and very nicely," he declared,
stroking her breasts.

Turning in his arms to face him, Maude slipped her arms
around his neck and pulled him down to her so they could finally

kiss in the way they had been longing to do. Pulling slightly away, Maude looked into her husband's eyes and said quietly, "And I have a surprise for you, just like the Saskatchewan soldier will surprise his bride with his gopher ranch."

"What? You're not going to make a fool of me, are you?"

"No, Will. I'm going to make a papa of you. I'm pretty sure I've been carrying our baby with me on this trip."

"Really? You mean we timed it just right in London?" Will asked in shock.

Somewhat concerned with the surprise in his voice, Maude confirmed, "Yes, Will, we did. I haven't seen a doctor yet, but I'm pretty sure. I hope it's okay with you."

"Okay?!" he exclaimed. "I'm thrilled!" With that he pulled her close, lifted her into his arms, and laid her gently in the bed. Crawling in beside her, he declared, "You couldn't have brought me a better gift. You were all I needed and wanted, but this addition makes our love complete."

After blissfully affirming their love, devotion, and future, Will and Maudie fell asleep in each other's arms.

CHAPTER
EIGHT

The next morning, Will took his bride out to his family's farm west of town. Maudie was greeted with warmth and affection by his parents, Thomas and Ellen Ryan. "Will has told us so much about you, Maudie," his mother, Ellen, said. "Oh, it is okay that we call you Maudie, isn't it? I understand your name is Maude, but Will refers to you as Maudie with such love in his eyes. We are very grateful that he has found such happiness again. Thank you, Maude."

Maude grinned and reached out her arms to Ellen. "Of course it's all right to call me Maudie. I love that he has chosen it as a pet name for me." She paused, then frowning added, "What should I call you, Mrs. Ryan?"

Laughing, Ellen replied, "Definitely not Mrs. Ryan. Ellen is fine. Maybe someday you'll feel comfortable calling me Mum. I understand you lost your own. I know I can't replace her, but I would like to support you like I know she would have."

"Thank you, Ellen. I appreciate that. And yes, my mother did pass away from the Flu Pandemic after World War I. Well, not right then, but even after the pandemic had declined, some individual cases of the flu popped up years later. I'm afraid my mother was one of those who succumbed to the disease." Tears filled Maudie's eyes.

"I'm so sorry, Maudie," Ellen said, drawing Maude into her aging arms for a hug. "I know you will miss your father and brothers, too. I hope they will come to visit your new home. They will always be welcome here. Well, maybe not here at the farm exactly. We're getting to the point where we probably can't handle it much longer, and since Will has no interest in taking it over, we will probably sell it and move to town."

"Oh, it would be wonderful to have you closer. I just thought of what I can call you: Grandma." At Ellen's quizzical look, Maude continued, saying, "I just let Will know last night that we are going to have a baby."

"How exciting!" Ellen exclaimed, pulling Maude into her arms again.

"What's going on?" Will asked as he and his dad entered the kitchen after surveying the changes that had occurred on the farm during Will's absence overseas.

"Tom!" Ellen cried out in excitement, letting go of Maude. "We're going to be grandparents!"

"What? Is that right, Will?" Tom asked, looking at his son.

"Yes, I guess it is, though Maudie hasn't seen a doctor yet, and she must as soon as possible."

"Oh, yes," Ellen agreed, suddenly looking downcast and worried. "We must look after our girl."

"Right!" Tom declared firmly. "One thing that's changed in our little town since you've been gone is that we now have a hospital, and Doc Adams has a couple of young fellows to help him."

"Oh, that is good news!" Will stated, putting his arm around Maude, who smiled sweetly and confidently at them, realizing all the sad memories they must be recalling about the loss of Will's first wife in childbirth.

Changing the direction of the conversation, Will said, "We'd better get going, Maudie. Ed and his wife, Nora, have invited us for afternoon tea, but knowing them, it may turn into something more spirited."

"I'm looking forward to meeting Nora and, of course, little Billy." Turning to Ellen and Tom, she said, "And it was so wonderful meeting you two. I hope we get to spend a lot of time together."

"Us, too," Tom stated as his wife hugged Maudie once again.

* * *

Climbing the stairs to the Stevenses' suite above the hardware store, Maude, breathing a bit heavily, said, "I love your parents, Will. They were so welcoming and kind to me. I hope Ed's wife will like me."

"Who wouldn't like you?" Will grinned, patting his wife's bottom as he climbed the stairs behind her. Will kept his concerns about Nora's reception of his new wife to himself, keeping in mind that she had been best friends with his first one.

As they reached the top of the stairs, Maude gave him a playful whack on his arm and said, "Oh, you. Not everyone thinks like you do." By then, Will was rapping on the door to the suite.

Ed opened the door and, bypassing his buddy, grabbed Maude in a bear hug, saying, "Welcome to Canada, Maudie! How are Larry and John, and your dad, Joe? Bet they're missing their girl. They were so good to us at Roberts Roost. Is the pub still open?"

"Hi, Ed. So good to see you. Yes, the pub is keeping them all busy, though Dad is stepping back from it more and more." Looking over his shoulder, Maude saw a small woman with brown curly hair and frowning brown eyes watching this greeting. Stepping back out of Ed's arms, she said, "I'm so anxious to meet Nora and wee Billy."

Turning around, Ed frowned and nodded at the woman, sending her the message to shape up, then said, "This is my wife, Nora. Nora, this is Will's Maudie that I've told you about."

Not moving, Nora acknowledged her with coolness in her voice. "Hello, Maude," she said, not using Will's pet name of affection. Then hearing the rambunctious voices of the two boys in the corner playing with a truck, she turned toward them and said, "The little one is our Billy, and the bigger one is his cousin, Little John."

"Oh, they're so cute and having such fun," Maude commented. She then noticed a young couple sitting on a couch next to where the boys were playing.

The young woman, who had long straight blondish hair, smiled, popped off the couch, and moved toward Maude with outstretched arms. "Welcome Maudie. I'm Alma, Nora's little sister. Well, younger sister. I'm actually taller than she is." She laughed, gave Maude a quick hug, then turned to the boys. "Come on, you two. Come and greet Will's bride."

Little John got up and came over to Maude with an outstretched hand. Shaking hers, he said, "Hello, Mrs. Ryan."

"Hello, John. You are a such a little gentleman."

"Thanks. But I'm not little. I'm five years old, going on six. Billy's the little gentleman."

At that, Billy popped up and ran over to John. Pushing him out of the way and copying his cousin, he said, "Hi. I'm Billy, and I'm two years old, going on three."

Leaning down to Billy, Maude smiled at both boys. "Hello, fellows. I'm so happy to meet you." Looking at their mothers and patting Billy on his blond head, she added, "They are such cute little sausages, and so polite." Seeing the women frowning at her, Maude explained that "little sausage" was just a term of endearment for children.

At that point, the tall, dark, good-looking man rose from the couch and introduced himself as John Leigh, Alma's husband and Little John's dad. Maude would learn that John had come to Crocus Plains several years ago and opened a drugstore. Alma, still in high school, had worked in Leigh's Drugstore on weekends and during summer vacation. They'd fallen in love, and soon after Alma's graduation, they'd married. Within a year they'd had John Daniel, thus explaining why he was older than his cousin Billy though his mother was younger than Aunt Nora. Named after his father, he became known as Little John.

The boys returned to playing with their trucks. Just as Will had predicted, Ed got the guys a beer, and the women gathered around the kitchen table with tea. Alma and Maude seemed to strike up an immediate friendship, discovering they were the same age and both expecting a baby. Nora remained somewhat aloof.

As the younger women discussed baby equipment, Alma asked Nora if Maudie could use Billy's baby carriage since she'd need the one she'd used for Little John.

Maude frowned. "What's a baby carriage? Is it something you use to carry a baby in your arms?" she asked, folding her arms together and rocking them.

Alma chuckled while Nora, with some disgust in her tone, explained, "It's like a bed on wheels that you can push your baby around in while walking."

"Oh, I know. You mean a perambulator, or pram!" Maude exclaimed, pleased she'd caught on.

"No," Nora replied sternly. "I mean a baby carriage." Maude bowed her head to take a sip of her tea. Nora then continued. "Come on, Alma, we need to get some cucumber sandwiches ready for tea and get the guys away from their beer."

As Alma moved reluctantly to join her sister, Maude went over to the boys and crouched down to play with them.

"You're being rather rude, aren't you, Nora?" Alma accused her sister.

"Well, you know Grace was my best friend, and this marriage with a baby on the way just seems too soon."

"Are you sure that's the only reason?" Alma asked, raising an eyebrow.

Ignoring her comment, Nora commanded, "Get the china tea set out of the cabinet and set the table."

As Alma set the table, she smiled to herself, watching Maude with the boys, who were laughing at her calling them "little sausages."

"Okay, everybody to the table," Nora called, placing a plate of sandwiches, pickles, and Nanaimo bars on the table.

While eating and chatting, the conversation turned to the Stevenses' apartment. Ed commented, "We're finding the place a little too small now with Billy, and being on the main drag above a store, there's no yard for him to play in. So we've talked to the Harrises, and since you aren't using their little house across the tracks, we've decided to buy it. It will be close for me to walk to work at the elevator and close to downtown for Nora and Billy to pick up a few groceries while out for a walk."

They all agreed it was a good idea. The afternoon closed on a happy note, with Nora even warming up a bit to Maude. Thus began a close relationship among the three young couples.

CHAPTER
NINE

With Little John having started school that fall, the three young women and Billy met at Wing Ling's Wok, a Chinese restaurant, a week after their meeting at the Stevenses'. Because many Chinese immigrants had been involved in building the trans-Canada railway lines, almost all small towns in Canada—particularly those on the prairies—had a Chinese restaurant. Wing Ling's Wok was a favourite of tourists as well as the locals, and workers often took their coffee breaks there.

At their husbands' insistence and because it was typical of the times, Nora, Alma, and Maude did not work outside their homes, all three becoming stay-at-home mums. The three sat drinking coffee, munching on scones, and puffing on cigarettes. The negative impact smoking could have on pregnancies and the risk of upper respiratory infections in small children caused by secondhand smoke were unknown during these times. Billy was coughing a bit and waving his hand in front of his nose to redirect the smoke away from the air he was breathing. It would have been considered disrespectful, however, during these times for a child to complain to a parent about their smoking.

Maude had not smoked until coming to Canada. It seemed a way to connect with the other young women in town, and it did seem to help relieve some stress. Tapping out the butt of her cigarette in an ashtray, she asked, "Do either of you have another fag? I forgot my pack at home."

Alma and Nora looked at her, eyebrows knit together, asking a question without words.

"Oh, sorry. I slipped into British slang for a cig."

Laughing, Alma passed Maude her pack of Craven A's.

"Guess I'm still getting used to a lot of differences in my new home. Even shopping is different. I went into Foster's Foods the other day to get some hamburger. The butcher asked how much I wanted. Not knowing anything about pricing, I said maybe ten cents worth would do. He handed me a huge amount. I was gob-smacked! There was so much meat, I knew it would take eating every day for a week to consume it all. Wish we had a fridge. We're still using an icebox."

Ignoring Maude's story, Nora observed, "Well, you two are beginning to fill out."

Alma and Maude grinned at one another. "Yes, we are at that," Maude agreed. "We'll soon have to start wearing smocks."

"Then you won't be having coffee at Wing Ling's anymore or going out at all," Nora stated firmly.

"Why not?" Maude asked as Alma shook her head and leaned it into her hand, thinking, *Here we go.*

"It's quite inappropriate for a pregnant woman to be seen in public," Nora explained. "Don't ask why it is; it just is."

"Blimey, that sounds like poppycock to me," Maudie declared. As Nora and Alma tilted their heads and pulled their eyebrows together quizzically at her terms, Maude continued. "How will I get my groceries then?"

Alma jumped in this time, avoiding her sister's insensitivity, and explained. "You can call Foster's Foods with your order. Will can pick it up later, or sometimes they'll deliver it. You can run a tab and pay it in full at the end of each month."

Not quite understanding all the social rules of her new country, Maude was grateful when winter arrived. Although she was unused to all the snow, wind, and cold, she at least had a reason to stay indoors and not be seen in public in a smock. She didn't realize, though, that covered in layers of clothes, she wouldn't be seen outside in only a smock in winter anyway. The gals did get together once in a while at one another's homes to play cards or have tea. They also worked on baby quilts for the expected spring arrivals.

The guys, in the meantime, formed a curling team, picking up one of the new school physical education teachers to make a foursome. They played every Monday evening plus the odd weekend bonspiel in Crocus Plains or surrounding small towns. They especially enjoyed "bonspieling," since the term included more than the game itself. Having several beers was a big part of the competitive tournament activity.

Ed and Will occasionally did a little ice fishing on Jackfish Lake. They didn't have a little wooden house on the lake like the regular fishermen as they didn't come out often enough to make it worthwhile. Instead, they'd drive onto the frozen lake, use an auger to drill a hole in the ice, and drop their lines into it with a bobber floating on top. When the bobber started bobbing up and down in the water, they knew they had a catch. Meanwhile, they could stay warm in the car, watching the hole and bobber while they visited, snacked on crackers and cheese, and sipped hot chocolate from a thermos. They often brought Billy with them. He enjoyed being with his dad and Will. He'd made such a strong connection to Will that he wanted to call him Uncle Will, but Nora thought it wouldn't be appropriate because Billy had a real uncle in John Leigh and they all spent a lot of time together.

* * *

Before they knew it, spring had arrived, and Maude and Alma were counting the days to their expected due dates. They had both engaged Dr. Jones, one of the new doctors who had joined Doc Adams in his practice. Their babies would be some of the first ones born in the new hospital that had been built in Crocus Plains.

Regardless, Will couldn't help but be somewhat anxious when Maudie went into labour and told him it was time to go to the hospital. The memory of his loss of Grace and their baby in childbirth was difficult to ignore. He paced in the hallway while Maude was in the delivery room. This was before fathers were included in the birthing experience. He sighed in relief when he saw Dr. Jones come out of the delivery room with a huge smile on his face.

Holding out his hand to Will, the doctor said, "Congratulations. You have a healthy seven-pound, eight-ounce baby girl. She's doing well, and so is Maude. She did really well. Once they get her and the baby cleaned up, they'll take her to her room and you can see her. You can soon take a peek at your baby girl in the nursery."

"Thanks, Doc," Will said, shaking Dr. Jones's hand. He made his way down the hall to wait for Maude in her room. The nurse brought her in shortly after he'd arrived, helping her get tucked into the bed.

After the nurse left, Will went to the bedside, brushed Maude's hair back from her forehead, and kissed her on her lips. Looking up into his admiring eyes, Maude said, "I know you were worried, Will. But everything went well, and we have a beautiful little girl."

"If she's anything like her mother, she'll be gorgeous. Is there anything I can do for you?"

"I'd like to ask one favour," Maude said, to which he quickly replied, "Anything."

"I wondered if we could name her Penelope after my mother. It would mean so much to me to honour my memory of Mum."

"Of course," Will agreed. "I think that's a great idea."

"Thank you, love. I also thought we could give her your mother's name for her middle name."

"Penelope Ellen Ryan. I like it. Maybe a little auspicious for a little one. Perhaps we could call her Penny while she's little."

"Oh, Will. I love it! I'm glad this part was easy. I'm sure when we bring her home, life won't be so easy." Maude grinned, then yawned.

"You're tired, sweetheart. I'd better go and let you get some rest."

"All right. Don't forget to check on Penny before you go." They both chuckled at the thought of this new little person who had already captured their hearts.

Three days later, Alma joined Maude in the hospital. Her labour was a little longer and tougher, but she soon delivered an eight-pound baby girl. She and John named her Sheryl.

Thus began many years of friendship between Penny and Sheryl as they grew up together in Crocus Plains.

CHAPTER
TEN

The three families spent a lot of time together, and Little John and Billy seemed enchanted with the baby girls. Sheryl, of course, was Little John's baby sister, and their cousin, Billy, seemed to have adopted Penny. The parents were so pleased that the boys liked to take the girls for a ride in one of the carriages while the adults enjoyed a beer or glass of wine and caught up on one another's news.

On this particular day, the group was sitting at a picnic table at the bottom of a hill next to Jackfish Lake. The boys had once again taken the girls for a carriage ride, together pushing it up the hill past the cottages built along both sides of the gravel road. Suddenly, the parents heard screaming from the boys. "Oh no! Look what you've done! Sto-o-op! Help!"

Running to the bottom of the hill, Will, Ed, and John caught the carriage, which was careening down the hill's gravel road, bumping and swaying as it hit loose rocks. Little John and Billy were running behind the carriage, trying to catch up.

"What the hell happened?" John asked the boys when they reached the bottom. Alma bumped his arm with her elbow, letting him know his wording was not appropriate.

Little John replied while trying to catch his breath. "When we got to the top, Billy turned the carriage around and let it go. I think it was an accident."

Fighting back tears, Billy explained further, "I was thinking what fun it would be to ride the carriage down the hill, so I thought Sheryl and Penny might like the thrill of the ride."

Having joined the group, Nora grabbed Billy and shouted, "They are babies, not adventurous young boys! Do you realize what a disaster this could have been?!"

"They're just kids themselves, Nora. Billy's only three, and at six, John isn't much older. Don't be too hard on them." Looking at the boys, who were choking back sobs, Ed added, "I think they're punishing themselves."

"And we should be punishing ourselves," said Alma. "What were we thinking letting a three-year-old and a six-year-old take on such responsibility? We were too involved in our own pleasure to watch over these kids. I think it's time we broke this party up."

* * *

Three years later, the families were gathered at the cottage John and Alma had bought by the lake. Here they'd made a sandbox and put up a swing set so the little ones had safe places to play. A wooden staircase connected the slight decline from the lawn to the water where a boat was hooked to a dock. Because there was no real beach on which the kids could play or wade into the water, the parents would take the kids to the public beach near the hill.

Sheryl and Penny were now three years old. Billy was six and would start grade one in the fall. Little John was nine and entering grade four. The Leighs had decided that having two John Leighs in the family would become more confusing as time went on, so they decided to start calling Little John by his first and middle name initials, J.D. When little sister Sheryl called him his new nickname, it came out more like "Jady."

When the four weren't playing something all together, the girls liked to get the boys involved in their special interests. Sheryl loved stories and wanted to be able to read herself. "Jady! Come help me read this book," she said. Being nine, J.D. enjoyed showing off a bit by teaching her what he knew. They settled into the canopied double porch swing that sat on the lawn, facing the lake. They were soon engaged in reading *Mother Goose Nursery Rhymes*. While it appeared that at three, Sheryl could already read this book, J.D. suspected they'd been over the rhymes so often, she probably just had them memorized. He started to think they needed to tackle some other books, perhaps Little Golden Book fairy tales such as *Goldilocks and the Three Bears*, *The Three Little Pigs*, *The Little Engine That Could*, or *Cinderella*.

Penny, on the other hand, enjoyed working with her hands and creating things. Maude had bought her some plasticine, a clay used for modeling things. It came in only a few colours and didn't dry up, so after each session of modeling, Penny would squeeze the items together in a lump, keeping it ready for the next time. The colours of the plasticine thus blended together into a neutral muddy colour.

"Come on, Billy," Penny cried from the picnic table. "Let's make a zoo of animals." She knew that Billy wouldn't want to make the little dishes that she liked to create, pretending they were china for a tea party. Billy readily joined her and immediately began creating a lion.

Meanwhile, the parents relaxed on the porch of the cabin in wicker chairs, munching on cheese and crackers and sipping on beer and homemade Tom Collinses. "I hear your mum and dad are moving into town, Will," Ed commented.

"Yeah, they sold the farm to a neighbour, and they bought Uncle George's place across the street from ours."

"Where are George and Betty going to live?" Nora asked.

"Well, Uncle George has decided it's time to retire, and he and Aunt Betty want to spend more time with their daughters, Deb and Barb, and their families, so they're moving to Morden."

"What about the Case dealership?" John asked.

"Well, I guess he's leaving that to me. He made me a partner early on knowing that someday he would retire, so he wanted to leave the business in the hands of someone he could trust," Will explained.

"Great!" said Ed. "I guess we've both come into our own. The agent I've been working for at the elevator is going to work for the Canadian Wheat Board and is moving to Winnipeg. The head office of the United Grain Growers has offered the position of elevator agent to me."

"This calls for a toast!" said John, raising his bottle of Labatt's Blue to the other two guys.

"We're pretty lucky, eh, girls," said Alma, raising her glass of Tom Collins. "We married us some pretty ambitious, responsible guys. They're kind of sexy, too," she giggled.

"Here, here to that!" agreed Maudie, while Nora shook her head, slightly disgusted at the two younger women, but she raised her glass all the same to the three husbands.

"Guess it's time we were getting home. Tomorrow will be a long day 'cause I promised Mum and Dad I'd come out to the farm to help them get organized for the move," said Will.

"Okay, dear. It will be so nice to have your folks across the street so Penny can be close to and get to know her grandparents," Maude commented, then called, "Come on, kids! Time to pack up and go home." Turning to the adults, she added, "Pip, pip, cheerio, and all that rot."

Alma whispered to Nora before she could make a snide remark, "I think she just means goodbye."

The Ryans and the Stevenses all climbed into the 1948 Dodge Coupe Will had purchased when he'd realized he couldn't keep borrowing his uncle's car, which wasn't large enough to hold a family anyway.

On the way home, Billy and Penny, insisting they sit together, were squished in the back seat between their mothers. Teasing one another and playing silly made-up games, the two wiggled and squirmed and happily pushed one another back and forth until their mothers told them to knock it off or, as Maudie said, "Keep your bloody hands to yourselves." This made Nora and the kids look at her, noting that there was no blood anywhere. "Oh, sorry," Maudie sighed. "Just another Brit expression."

* * *

Penny loved being able to walk across the street to Grammy Ellen and Papa Tom's place to visit them. It was a larger house with a much larger yard than hers. The reddish-brown Insulbrick siding was a flat fiberboard sheathing stamped with a brick pattern. White-framed windows and a white front door porch accented the imitation brick siding.

A large square yard surrounded by crab apple trees ran to one side of the house. Penny loved to pick the crab apples with her Grandpapa, and she ate her share, even though the tartness wrinkled up her mouth and nose. Grammy was adept at turning this sour fruit into jams and jellies. Grammy also had a large garden behind the house, and she often engaged Penny in helping to weed the garden or pick and shell peas.

Beyond the garden, Papa had a shed where he liked to do woodwork. Penny sometimes visited him there, and she liked to play in the piles of sawdust on the floor. After a while, Grammy would call them in for afternoon tea. She'd have celery sticks filled with a spread made of Cheese Whiz and pimentos. There were always maple tarts and freshly baked oatmeal cookies. Grammy also let Penny have her own cup of tea in a miniature china cup and saucer that Grammy had bought especially just for her. The only unfortunate thing about teatime with her grandparents was that Grammy was a bit of a food-pusher; she was never convinced that Penny didn't want one more of something.

These times with Papa and Grammy gave Maudie the opportunity to run uptown to shop or to meet the gals for coffee at Wing Ling's Wok. Sometimes when Maudie and Alma had a UCW (United Church Women) meeting at the church, Sheryl would join Penny at her grandparents' place. The girls' imaginations turned the large square encompassed yard into the home of princesses as they pretended Cinderella's pumpkin carriage took them around the square. Grammy's many pots of beautiful geraniums, marigolds, and nasturtiums on the steps of the front porch created a beautiful throne. On each side of the porch railings, her rose bushes added to the image. The sidewalk from the steps to the street bordered by pansies, petunias, and portulaca, also known as moss roses, presented to the girls a walkway even more royal than a red carpet leading from a palatial throne.

One Sunday in the spring, Will decided to show Penny Pine Ridge, the country school he had attended, since it wouldn't be long before she'd be starting grade one in a very different environment. He also wanted to show her the wild prairie crocuses that grew out in the valley near the school. "Can Sheryl come with us, Daddy?" she asked. Will agreed as long as it was all right with her parents, the Leighs.

After showing the girls the little wooden one-room school house, Will explained that he'd walk or ride a horse the two miles from the farm to school in spring and fall, but in the winter, the kids would sometimes ride in a large wooden wagon with runners like a sled pulled by work horses. One year the teacher had given him a quarter a month to come early on winter mornings to start up the wood stove so the room would be warm for the other kids when they arrived. She warned him that he mustn't use kerosene to make the start-up easier because it would be too dangerous.

He then took the girls down the hill from the school to a little meadow in the valley. He soon found a patch of wild lilac-coloured crocuses and kneeled down to pick some. Handing one each to Penny and Sheryl, he said, "Feel the petals. See how fuzzy and hairy they are? That's what protects them in the spring if they sprout up a little too early, so they can survive a late snowfall and cold weather. They are the true sign of spring, and that's why Manitoba has chosen the crocus as its provincial flower."

"Oh, they're so pretty. Can we take some home to Mummy?" Penny asked.

"Me, too?" added Sheryl. "Can we grow these in our gardens?"

"Of course, girls, you can take some for your mothers," Will replied. "We'd have to come back when the plants go to seed to be able to plant any at home. I think they're more comfortable out here in the wild. That's why they are prairie crocuses rather than the bulb kind."

CHAPTER
ELEVEN

*A*fter three preschool years of creative play at Penny's grandparents' home had passed, she and Sheryl were now six and starting grade one. It was the 1950s, and there was no public kindergarten in those days. J.D., who was now twelve and in grade seven, walked them to the small white elementary school on Central Avenue in the same one-acre yard as the two-story stone high school. As Crocus Plains was growing, the elementary school was getting overcrowded, yet there was no room in the high school for the upper grades seven and eight. There was talk of building a new high school with room for the junior high grades as well.

At recess and lunchtime, fourth-grader Billy made sure he checked on Penny and his cousin Sheryl, pushing them on the swings and playing tag. The girls loved their teacher, Miss Norton, and both loving to learn, they were soon at the head of their class.

As they progressed through elementary school, it became evident that their interests and talents were still different. Sheryl loved reading—even if the school Dick and Jane series were boring—and she liked writing, too, so maybe one day she'd write her own book. Penny, on the other hand, was a whiz at math. They both did well in all the subjects and traded off being at the top of their classes. Unfortunately, the teachers during those days used this exchange to keep them motivated, writing things on their report cards about being only two or three percentage points ahead of the other. Nothing, however, would destroy their friendship.

Penny and Sheryl enjoyed recess even more as they developed and learned to skip. While the boys played catch or chased one another around the playground, many of the girls would line up on the sidewalk leading up to the school's entrance with long skipping ropes. A girl holding the rope at each end would turn the rope while one or two girls would run into the turning rope and jump. The rest of the girls waiting their turn would burst into skipping rhymes that helped the rhythm of the turning rope.

One day, Elonda and Lisa were turning the rope while Sheryl was jumping. The other girls started into a verse with a sing-song rhythm: "Bernie and Sheryl sitting in a tree, K-I-S-S-I-N-G. First comes love, then comes marriage, then comes Sheryl with a baby carriage."

"That will never happen!" Sheryl denied. The girls all burst out laughing while she escaped the rope and their teasing.

A little nervous about being next in line, Penny took her place at the rope's center. Elonda and Lisa began slowly turning the rope as the rest of the girls chimed, "Cinderella dressed in yella, went upstairs to kiss her fella. How many kisses did she give him?" Then they began counting in a very quick rhythm while Elonda and Lisa turned the rope faster. The counting quit when Penny stumbled and couldn't keep going. "Wow, you kissed him twelve times!" the girls yelled.

Sheryl and Penny decided it was time to move on to something else during recess when their friends decided to do Double Dutch skipping. That included two long ropes being turned in opposite directions with the skipper trying to jump each rope as it touched the ground.

The Leigh and Ryan families had invested in the new entertainment device of television. If the girls had to stay home from school because they were sick or there was a blizzard, their favourite pastime was watching the kids' programs *The Friendly Giant* and *Chez Hélène*. The tall giant told great stories with his puppet friends, Rusty the Rooster and Jerome the Giraffe. The French lady Hélène introduced the French language to English-speaking children, since French was also an official language of Canada. Though they enjoyed the show, Penny and Sheryl didn't always understand it.

The three families still got together on weekends. Sometimes they would be at the Leighs' cabin on Jackfish Lake, but other times they might go to the Stevenses' place, the little brick house across the tracks from Ed's elevator. The area between their street and the elevator was undeveloped and overgrown with grasses, weeds, and shrubs. Billy had made a fort in the center of it so the younger kids could enjoy playing there and have picnics. J.D. was getting more involved in sports like baseball, going to movies, and hanging out with his buddies, so he didn't hang out with the younger ones as much.

Another activity the younger three enjoyed together was going to the Case Farmers' Forum. Once a year, Will would host this special day for his customers or potential ones, sponsored by the Case equipment company, at his dealership. They would show films presenting the advantages of their products and introducing the new ones. A guest speaker would be present from the company to answer questions. There were delicious refreshments provided and served by Maudie with the help of Alma and Nora. After school, Penny, Sheryl, and Billy would walk down to the dealership to snack and go around to all the displays, picking up pamphlets to use for playing store in Billy's fort.

When Sheryl was in grade four, Alma went back to helping out part-time at Leigh's Drugstore. The Leighs had moved from the Ryans' neighbourhood when they'd bought a small brown bungalow on Central Avenue just south of the elementary school.

On days when Alma helped John at the store, Penny would walk home with Sheryl to her house to play. After a snack, they engaged in their favourite pastime, playing in Sheryl's bedroom with her many Barbies and their clothes. At some point, Sheryl would start singing, "It's Howdy Doody time," and indeed it was, so the girls would go to the living room and watch the Canadian version of *Howdy Doody* on their black-and-white television. The Leighs had also bought a small record player. Sheryl liked to sing, so after the television show, they'd play her mother's seventy-eights. One of their favourite songs was "True Love" sung by Bing Crosby and Grace Kelly.

* * *

Over the next couple of years, the community built a long new two-story high school in the far end of the same yard as the other schools. The old stone high school that Will and, more recently, J.D. had attended had been torn down. With the students from the country schools and small villages in the area being bussed now to Crocus Plains for high school, there was still no room in the new building for the seventh and eighth graders, so two portables were built behind the elementary school to house those grades. The new building, which included a gymnasium, took up a large portion of the north end of the schoolyard, so there was no longer room for a softball diamond. Any interest in the sport had to be fulfilled by the park board at the fields down in the fairgrounds near the lake.

Billy spent grade eight in one of the portables before moving on to grade nine in the new high school, which was called Crocus Plains Collegiate Institute. The school had taken on the same type of title most of the high schools on the prairies had adopted because it offered university entrance as well as general and business curriculums. J.D. would soon be graduating from CPCI.

Penny and Sheryl, meanwhile, were spending their last two years of elementary school in the little white building where they'd begun grade one.

Every morning the elementary students would line up in paired rows by grade outside the school when the bell rang. Penny and Sheryl were always partners in the lineup. The teachers would then come to the beginning of their class rows and lead them into school. These procedures were also used after lunch.

When the school would participate in the November 11 Remembrance Day service, the same organized process was used. Students would arrive as usual on that school day, but by ten o'clock, the teachers would have their classes lined up and they would march to the Town Hall. Each student wore a poppy, respectfully listened to the service, and sang the songs, including "O Canada" at the beginning and "God Save the Queen" at the end. Classes were then dismissed for the rest of the day. For both Penny and Billy, this day had great meaning because both of their fathers had participated overseas in World War II. Penny also knew that her mother, Maudie, had lived through the wartime experience as well. Penny herself had been a positive result of the war.

After-school television programs for the girls had advanced to *Fury* and *The Roy Rogers Show*. On weekends, along with their parents, they enjoyed watching *Father Knows Best* and *Leave It to Beaver*. Before they got a television, Penny's family always had the radio on during their Sunday dinner, which was usually a pot roast from which leftovers could be used for supper all week. There were programs that were like plays but could only be heard, not seen. Some of their favourites, *Father Knows Best* and *Our Miss Brooks*, then became television shows.

A library had opened in town, and both girls had cards. Even Penny enjoyed some of the books they could borrow, like *Heidi* and *Anne of Green Gables*.

In the summers following grades five and six, Penny and Sheryl would often spend the day at the beach. Meeting at the schoolyard, they'd walk to the south end of town, over the bridge between the bay and the lake, and through the park to the beach. J.D. was usually there lifeguarding during his high school and college years, so their parents felt safe letting the girls go on their own. It was a time when children—especially in small towns— had a lot of freedom. Billy often showed up, too, and talked to J.D., wanting to grow up like his cousin and do everything he did. He would show off a little to the girls by running down the pier and jumping off the diving board.

One day while Sheryl was talking to her brother, Penny was looking longingly at the raft that floated at least twenty-five yards from the shore. "What's up? A penny for your thoughts," Billy said, chuckling at his pun as he came up behind her.

Not understanding what he meant, she cocked her head, frowning at him as she responded. "Oh, I've always wanted to swim out to the raft, but I'm worried I might not make it. I can swim, but I've never had lessons."

Grabbing her hand, Billy said, "Come on. I know you can do it, and I'll swim beside you all the way." And that they did, climbing onto the raft to sit and chat for a while before swimming back to shore.

There was many a Saturday morning that Penny and Sheryl would take off on their pedal bikes with a sack lunch and ride down to a big old oak tree with huge low-hanging branches in a vacant lot. They'd climb into the crook of a branch and sit and talk most of the day, snacking on their lunch midday.

"What do you think about boys?" Sheryl asked.

"What do you mean? What's to think about them?" Penny responded.

"I've been wondering when it is that girls and boys start getting interested in one another. I sometimes wonder if my cousin Billy is interested in you."

Penny's eyes perked up. "Really? He's too bloody old for me, and I'm sure there're lots of girls in junior high after him."

"True," Sheryl agreed. "But someday soon, he might not be too old. What do you mean by bloody?"

"Oh, it's just an expression. I think I'm picking up some of my mum's British phrases. By the way, your brother J.D. is tall, dark, and handsome just like your dad." Penny paused. "I've often wondered why Billy is so fair when his dad and even your Aunt Nora both have brown hair and eyes."

"Oh, J.D.'s way too old for you," Sheryl interrupted Penny.

"Maybe he could wait for me to grow up," Penny mused. "Anyway, we better get going home. Our mums don't worry about us unless we don't show up for supper."

* * *

By grades five and six, boys had become a bit of an interest to Penny and Sheryl, and boys were becoming a little interested in them. They had a strange way of showing it though. At recess in the winter when fresh snow covered the school playground, the boys would chase the girls around the yard and tackle them so they both would fall into the snow. There was no playground supervision during these times, so Billy would sometimes sneak over to the elementary playground to check on the girls and protect them if needed. One day, however, he kind of forgot himself and tackled Penny. "What the heck are you doing, dingbat?" Penny shouted at him as she pushed herself off the ground and brushed the snow off her parka and snow pants. Secretly, she thought maybe it was because he liked her.

Skating was a favourite winter pastime in small prairie towns. Penny and Sheryl would often walk across town together, skates over their shoulders, to the indoor rink for public skating on Tuesday or Thursday evenings and Saturday or Sunday afternoons. Skating round and round the perimeter, they would giggle when the boys would try cutting them off. "Why don't they just ask us to skate with them?" Sheryl asked Penny.

"Oh, they're too chicken for that. If only we could ask them," Penny replied.

"Yeah. That would be cool. But, of course, our mums wouldn't approve. That wouldn't be ladylike. Girls don't do that." Their mothers as members of the Royal Purple, an auxiliary of the Elks Lodge at the time, were often at the rink to run the concession stand.

By eighth grade, the boys would sometimes cruise by a little closer and either try to grab their toques or mitts to get the girls to chase them. Because the boys were now into hockey, Penny and Sheryl often walked to the rink on a weeknight or weekend to watch them play. They were particularly interested in watching Roger and Bernie from their class. Billy was with the Midget Park Board team of high schoolers, so they'd sometimes go to those games with their parents. J.D. had been interested in hockey, too, but he had graduated and left home, attending Assiniboine Community College in Brandon.

In their eighth-grade classroom, Sheryl sat in front of Penny near the back of the room in an outside row. Their wooden desks had drawers under the seats. Bernie would often come over and pull out the drawer on Penny's desk and sit down to chat while they were doing their math assignments. One day, after he'd sat down and they were talking about one of the problems, Roger came over, too, and leaned on the other side of Penny's desk. After the boys went back to their own desks, Sheryl turned around and said to Penny, "Aren't you Miss Popularity today!" then added, "They only like you because you're so smart in math."

Penny looked up at Sheryl, frowning. Sheryl started to laugh and patted her friend's hand. "I'm only kidding, Penny. They like you because you're a great gal and pretty. You're smart, too."

Smiling back at Sheryl and realizing her friend would never hurt her, Penny laughed, too, and said, "Well, you know who they come to for help with literature now that we're studying Shakespeare. At least it's better than when we were in grade five and the boys sitting behind us would dip our ponytails in their inkwells in the corner of their desks."

"Yeah," Sheryl agreed. "At least your hair didn't show the blue ink. I'd have to walk around all day with a blue tip on my blond ponytail."

On Saturday afternoons, they'd often go to the afternoon matinee at the Rainbow Theatre. They usually stopped at the bus depot first to pick up a sack of penny candy or saved their fifty-cent allowances to buy popcorn and a Coke at the theatre. Those were the days when fifty cents would get one into the show and get the snacks, too.

They loved Elvis Presley hits, such as *Blue Hawaii* and *G.I. Blues*. The *Tammy and the Bachelor* and *Gidget* series had also grabbed their interest earlier and continued to be favourites with each new film. The *Beach Party* ones with Frankie Avelon and Annette Funicello soon became their ultimate favourites. Sheryl especially loved the music in films, and Penny had to hold her back from bursting into song. In later high school years, Penny, on the other hand, became attracted to Westerns with good-looking cowboys like Clint Eastwood.

Church had also played a significant role in their growing-up years. Both girls attended Sunday school at the United Church throughout their elementary years and briefly attended an after-school program called Explorers that Maudie had started with some other young mothers. During their junior high years, they'd don their white and navy-blue trimmed middies after school to go to the United Church as members of CGIT. Canadian Girls in Training was a Christian nondenominational group formed to promote leadership skills, social responsibility, and the care for world humanity in girls in grades seven to twelve. They enjoyed creative and athletic activities based on protestant Christian values. Penny and Sheryl had considered Girl Guides, but they had opted for CGIT instead.

* * *

It was the 1960s, and Penny and Sheryl were just finishing grade eight and anticipating their move into high school. At the end of June every school year there was an elementary field day. All the small village and country schools came to Crocus Plains to participate in a sports day, including track and field events. The day, however, began with a parade down Central Avenue to the fairgrounds. Each school's students dressed in costumes and either marched or rode on floats, depending on the size of the school. Crocus Plains, being the largest school, practiced for weeks, its students marching in long military-style formation. They wore black uniforms, the boys in black pants and white shirts, the girls in black tunics and white blouses. Two eighth-grade girls got to carry the Crocus Plains banner and got to wear cream skirts and lilac-coloured tops representing the lilac-coloured crocuses.

This year, the banner carriers were Sheryl and Penny. "Isn't this neat?" Sheryl commented to Penny, who responded, "Yeah, as Mum would say, we're the bee's knees. We've come a long way from riding the Holland-themed float in first grade dressed as little Dutch girls."

Looking at one another, they said simultaneously, "And what will next year bring?"

Over the summer, they spent more time listening to the current hits on their transistor radios as they walked to the beach and park by the lake. Sheryl would beg Penny to sing along with her as they'd walk along, and passing cars would hear their rendition of the Dixie Cups' "Chapel of Love" and Dusty Springfield's "Wishin' and Hopin'." The English rock and roll band the Beatles had also hit the North American airwaves, so "She Loves You," "All My Loving," and "I Want to Hold Your Hand" also became a part of their repertoire.

Chapter
TWELVE

It was the first day of grade nine. Maudie was packing a sack lunch for Penny while Will helped her organize her schoolbag with all the new scribblers and a plastic zippered case holding pens, pencils, and a pencil sharpener. He slipped her a couple of dollars for an emergency and concluded, "Well, as your mum would say, everything is tickety-boo."

Adding the sack lunch to Penny's schoolbag, Maudie said, "I think they are starting to provide school lunches now at the high school, so maybe look into that and we can send the money for your tickets. I guess more kids stay over the noon hour in high school because they can participate in activities. I'll miss your walking home every day for lunch now." Putting her hands one each side of Penny's cheeks, Maudie kissed her daughter on her forehead. "I'm sure everything will be hunky-dory."

"I hope so, Mum. I'm a little anxious."

"I'll give you a ride today so you don't mess up your new dress that Mum made or trip on your new shoes," Will said, putting his arm around his little girl.

Penny smiled to herself, remembering their recent trip to Brandon to shop for shoes. They made the trip twice a year, in the spring and the fall, for new shoes for the season. They probably wouldn't have to go as often now that her growth was slowing down. What made her smile was remembering when she and

Maudie had gone to the washroom in Eaton's, the big department store. As they'd approached the washroom, Maudie had reminded Penny to put a piece of toilet paper across the seat to prevent picking up any germs from previous users—a common practice that even when she became an adult, Penny continued to do it out of habit, regardless of research. It was the next step that had made Penny grin to herself after her dad's comment. In order to use a stall, one had to put a dime in the door slot box to unlock it. While they were in adjoining stalls, Penny heard her mum say a little verse: "Here I sit, brokenhearted. Paid a dime and only farted."

"Mum!" Penny cried out, laughing. "I can't believe you said that!"

"Oops. Sorry if I embarrassed you, but no one else is in here." Then, as they both came out of their stalls, they saw two women waiting to go in, chuckling to themselves. Fortunately, they had a good sense of humor and appreciated Maudie's creativity, nodding in agreement that this was often the case.

Will dropped Penny off on Central Avenue near the front of the school, where Sheryl was waiting for her so they could face their first day together. They were both dressed in colourful shifts their mothers had made from hopsacking, a coarsely woven cotton.

Penny's was patterned in autumn flowers and leaves in bright shades of orange, red, rust, yellow, and brown. It accented her shoulder-length brunette curls with reddish-blond highlights, a combination of her parents' colouring. But it was her mother's warm brown eyes that shone with kindness. Long shoulder-length honey-blond curls framed Sheryl's fair complexion. Her shift sported polka dots in blue, magenta, and purple.

As they walked toward the school entrance, both girls attracted the attention of some of the older boys lining the sidewalk. A few wolf whistles burst out. Billy, standing next to a couple of the whistlers, nudged them with his elbows and said emphatically, "Knock it off, jerks. That's my cousin and her best friend." Others heard him, too, and since no one messed with Billy, they all toned down.

This was Freshie week, which meant all the ninth graders would be hazed on Friday. They'd have to wear a costume that the upper levels suggested, and they'd each be assigned as a slave to a senior-level student for Friday. Billy had decided then and there that he'd make sure Sheryl and Penny were assigned to him.

Penny and Sheryl luckily were assigned to the same homeroom with Mr. Benson. Their friends Roger and Bernie were in the same class, but most of the others were unfamiliar, so they were probably bussed-in students. By the end of the week, they had already made friends with Diane and Marsy, who came on the bus from north of Crocus Plains.

When Friday rolled around, the girls showed up at the Stevenses' house across the tracks in their Freshie Day costumes as babies. They were to come in large diapers made by wrapping a sheet around their bottoms, along with wearing a large cardboard bib over their T-shirts. Since Billy had them assigned to him as his slaves, they were to arrive at his house prior to the start of the school day to wash the Stevenses' car with toothbrushes. Though this was a long, monotonous chore, Billy felt that it kept the girls from worse prospects. When they were finished, he drove them to school. The day was filled with a lot of nonsense and not a lot of concentration on classwork.

That evening was their first high school dance. Billy planned to go, too, as this would be his last year of school dances, so he said he'd drive them rather than their having to walk or get their dads to drive them. He picked up Penny first because she lived closer to him and Sheryl's house was closer to the school.

He was climbing out of his family car when Penny walked out the back door of the Ryans' home. His eyes widened and he sucked in his breath as this beautiful girl walked toward him in a pink taffeta sleeveless dress with a wide stand-up collar that crossed her collarbone to each side of her shoulders. The bodice fit snuggly to her waistline, at which point the skirt flared slightly to her knees. The bangs of her loosely curled reddish-brunette hair were parted in the center, framing her face and blending in with the lengthy waves that flowed down each side of her neck and onto her upper chest. When had she grown up?

Will had followed his daughter out of the house. Maudie was across the street, taking care of his mother, Ellen, who hadn't been feeling well. They had lost his father, Tom, over the summer to a heart attack.

Looking at Billy, Will said, "I expect you to watch over her and bring her home safely."

"Of course, Will. I remember all the ethics and manners you taught us in Boy Scouts," Billy responded. He had the highest respect and regard for Will, who not having sons of his own, had taken on the job of Scoutmaster a few years ago. As his godson and Ed's son, Billy had always held a special place in Will's heart.

"I'm going to go check on your Grammy Ellen. Have a good time, you two," Will said as he turned to go across the street to his mother's house.

Billy smiled down at Penny as he opened the passenger door for her. She smiled back at him, thinking he looked pretty attractive in his khaki dress pants and turquoise shirt, which brought out the blue in his eyes and complemented his sandy hair. Again, she wondered how he was so fair when his parents were much darker.

When they arrived at the Leighs' home, Sheryl dashed out in a formfitting turquoise taffeta dress overlapped with a full chiffon draping tent. Her honey-blond hair barely touched her shoulders in a smooth pageboy. Frowning, Billy tilted his head, wondering, *When did my little cousin grow up, too?*

It didn't take long to go the block and a half down the street to the high school. When they entered the gymnasium, the DJ was playing the Beatles' version of "Twist and Shout."

"Let's go!" said Penny, grabbing Sheryl's hand, and they raced over to join a group of girls, including their new friends Diane and Marsy, and immediately started shifting the balls of their feet back and forth along with their hips in time to the music. Facing one another, Sheryl and Penny continued to shift and wiggle as they squatted their bodies down toward the floor and back up again. As they continued twisting upright, they bent their elbows and, forming fists with their hands, shifted them back and forth in time to the music, once in a while circling their hands as they shifted them.

Standing with his buddies on the sidelines, Billy was surprised at their dancing talent, but his friends were more attracted by their lovely forms. "Who are those babes, Bill?" one of them asked.

"That's my cousin and her best friend. Keep your eyes and hands off them!"

"Okay! Okay!" they all responded, shaking their hands in the air. "At least until you're not around!" one of them added, chuckling, and the others joined in.

The music had changed then to regular rock, and the girls in the circle started doing their own thing to the tempo. Billy joined them to keep an eye on Sheryl and Penny. The girls, noticing that most of the guys were just hanging out by the sides, waved at Bernie and Roger to join them, which they did.

When the music slowed to a waltz tempo, Bernie and Roger got Penny and Sheryl to partner up with them. Billy was relieved that the girls were with their friends and not left open to his friends. After a variety of rock and waltzes, the last dance of the evening was, of course, a slow waltz. At that point, Diane, who had been chosen Freshie Queen, cut in on Penny and Bernie, who was Freshie King, leaving Penny vulnerable to whoever might approach. Fortunately, it was Billy, and he cuddled her gently as they slid to the final Beatles' song of the evening, "This Boy." It was a romantic song, and Billy couldn't help but feel that this boy wanted to draw Penny a little closer, but remembering Will, he kept a respectable distance like a gentleman should.

After the dance, Billy dropped his cousin off first, then headed for Penny's house. On the way, they talked about their plans for the weekend. Billy said he had to help his dad at the elevator, coopering cars on Saturday.

"What's that?" Penny asked.

"Oh, it's preparing boxcars for shipping grain by train to the shipyards, where boats are loaded to take our grain to other parts of the country or other countries. Since it's fall harvest time, I also have to go out to check the moisture content of some of the farmers' crops."

"How would you do that?"

"Come along and I'll show you how I do it. We can go Sunday afternoon after church."

"Okay," Penny agreed. "I didn't know you did all that for your dad at the elevator."

By this time, they'd reached Penny's house. Billy got out, opened the car door for her, and walked her to the kitchen door. He looked into her eyes and started to lean down, then abruptly rose and, going back to the car, called, "See you Sunday about one o'clock."

Tilting her head quizzically, Penny thought, *I think he was going to kiss me. I wonder why he didn't.*

The kitchen door then opened, and Will pulled his daughter inside, asking how the dance was. After her brief description, she looked at her parents, who weren't really listening, but were patting one another's backs as if comforting each other. "Is something the matter?" Penny asked.

"We're worried about your Grammy Ellen, sweetie," Maudie replied. "She was in such pain tonight, we had to take her to the hospital. We're not sure what's going on, but it seems serious."

"Oh no!" Penny choked out, tears forming in her eyes.

Her dad hugged her and said, "It's in the doctors' and God's hands now. I think we best go to bed and say our prayers."

* * *

The next day, Will and Maudie skipped church to go to the hospital to check on Will's mother. Penny went to church and met Billy, and he brought her to his home for lunch. Nora didn't seem overly thrilled with the idea, but Ed welcomed Penny and asked about her grandma, wishing her well.

After lunch, Billy and Penny drove into the country, stopping at large wheat fields. The sun shone brightly on the fields, and a light breeze created golden waves in the grain. Pulling off to the side of the road, Billy got out of the car and walked a short way into the field. Snapping off the heads from some stalks of grain, he placed the heads in the palm of one hand and crushed them back and forth with the other until the kernels of grain fell out of their pockets. He then blew the husks away, leaving the bare kernels.

"Yep. This crop looks ready to go. They'll probably be harvesting soon. Do you want some gum?" he asked Penny, who had come up beside him.

"Maybe. What kind have you got?"

Laughing at her innocent ignorance, he explained, "If you chew these kernels long enough, it becomes a natural gum. Here, give it a try."

"Really?" Penny questioned as she took the kernels out of his hand.

"Really. We better get going. I've got a couple more fields to check."

"You seem to know a lot about grain," Penny noted, chewing steadily on the kernels. "Are you going to work with your dad in the elevator when you graduate?"

"No. I don't think it's for me, especially when I have to meet up with rats when crawling through the boot, cleaning up the grain that has leaked into it from the pit above. I'm going to apply to Assiniboine Community College in Brandon to take a mechanics course. I'm thinking that this summer instead of helping Dad in the elevator, I might ask Will—uh, your dad— if I can work with him at the Case dealership. He's a fantastic mechanic, and I think I could learn a lot from him. That way I won't feel completely out of place at school."

"Didn't J.D. take that course?" Penny asked.

"Yeah, he did, but then he signed up with the military, and he's out at Shilo now for basic training. His mechanic's background should help him get good positions with the Army."

"Sheryl said he met a girl at Assiniboine, and she thinks it's kind of serious."

Billy nodded in agreement, "Yeah, he did. I think her name is Stella. She was taking a secretarial course. She's from Minnedosa. That's probably why we don't see him much anymore."

"Guess he's not going to wait for me to grow up."

"What?" Billy looked at her with shock and disbelief in his eyes.

"Gotcha!" Penny giggled. "I was just kidding. I know he's too old for me, but I always thought he was a good-looking guy."

"He's a good guy, too," Billy added. "Stella got herself a great catch."

"Maybe you'll find yourself a winner at college." Penny grinned.

Frowning and ignoring her comment, Billy said, "We'd better get back to town. It's almost suppertime. Your folks will be expecting you, and you'll want to find out about your grandma."

Chapter
THIRTEEN

Two months later, Penny sat with her parents in the front row of the United Church at her Grammy Ellen's funeral. Grammy Ellen had developed stomach cancer, and though she'd had surgery and treatment, she hadn't survived. Tears dripped down Penny's cheeks as she listened to Sheryl sing "Softly and Tenderly," one of her grandma's favourite songs, which was very appropriate for her journey "home."

At the reception following the service and burial, Sheryl and Penny embraced one another in a lingering hug, with Sheryl's feeling sad for her friend and Penny's being grateful for Sheryl sharing her talent in honour of Grammy Ellen.

Losing her Grammy Ellen just before the Christmas season was about to begin was especially tough for Penny. They'd always had Christmas dinner at her grandparents' place. She knew things would be different when they had lost Papa Tom last summer, but now they were both gone. She'd never be able to run across the street to their house for a snack after school again. What was going to happen to Grammy's house?

As it happened, Will had discussed that very issue with his siblings, who'd come back to Crocus Plains for their mother's funeral. They'd all agreed that he should take over the house because he'd taken care of its maintenance for his folks in their later years. It was also bigger than the little house his own family lived in across the street, and he'd been thinking about looking for a bigger place. Taking over his parents' house would feel like home for him and his family, though the memories might linger and be difficult to deal with for a while.

* * *

While her parents spent the rest of the fall making the move across the street, Penny and Sheryl began exploring school activities. Diane and Marsy had wanted them to join them as cheerleaders, but Penny and Sheryl didn't think cheerleading was for them. It was natural for Sheryl to join the choir. Mr. Benson, the girls' homeroom and math teacher, had convinced Penny that the art club he supervised would be a good choice for someone as talented in math as she was. He explained that the concept of space relationships in art corresponded with those in geometry. Having always enjoyed working with her hands as a child, Penny thought she would give it a try. Both she and Sheryl were soon very engaged in their groups, but they never let them interfere with their friendship.

The weekend after the Canadian fall harvest Thanksgiving, the final football game of the season was being played. Penny and Sheryl attended the game to watch their cheerleading friends and Roger, who was the team's quarterback. Bernie sat with them on the bleachers, his eyes as much on the cheerleaders as they were on his friend Roger.

"How come you didn't try out for the football team?" Penny asked Bernie.

"I'm saving my energy for my favourite sport, hockey," he responded.

"Oh," Sheryl joined in. "Is Roger going to play, too? We always liked watching you guys the past couple of years."

"Yeah, I think so. Roger's into all sports. I wish we had a high school hockey team like they do in the States. Wouldn't have to worry about getting rides to games in other parts of the province."

Suddenly, the crowd was on its feet cheering. Roger had scored a touchdown, and the CPCI Wildcats had won the game. The cheerleaders stood behind Roger, facing the fans, and did their favourite cheer, adjusting the last line because of the team's win. They kicked out their legs in rhythm with the words: "We've got the T-E-A-M that's on the B-E-A-M. We've got the team that's on the beam, that's really hip to the jive. Way to go, Wildcats! You skinned them alive!" They then surrounded Roger, hugging him.

"Hmmm," said Bernie, watching the happenings. "Maybe I should have joined football. It's a good thing they decided to call our teams the Wildcats instead of the Crocus Cats. Can't you just imagine the opposition referring to them as the Pussy Cats?" The girls laughed at his joke as Bernie got up to leave the bleachers. Turning to Penny and Sheryl, he said, "See you gals later at the dance."

Penny and Sheryl waited for Diane and Marsy to change out of their cheerleading outfits. Billy waited with them because he was going to give them a ride to Sheryl's house. Diane and Marsy were staying overnight in town so they could go to the Harvest Dance. All four girls decided to make a girls' night of it, and they were staying at Sheryl's because they could walk to the gym easily from there. The adults were all going to spend the evening at the Ryans'. The three couples had been making a routine of meeting at one another's places one night a week to play Rummoli and, of course, imbibe in spirited refreshments.

After the four girls ate the light supper Sheryl's mother Alma had left for them, they began helping one another create the most current hairstyles. Marsy wanted a beehive, so Sheryl was back-combing her whole head before smoothing the top layer with a comb, pulling it all together at the back, and fastening it with bobby pins at her neck.

Sheryl then brushed her own hair back behind her ears and twisted it up into a roll held together with bobby pins. Marsy commented, "Hey, you're great at making a French Twist," as she fastened a pretty velvet bow along the side of the roll for Sheryl.

Meanwhile, Diane brushed the top of Penny's hair back and formed a roll on the back of her head with part of her hair, then brushed the rest down to her shoulders. She attached a plaid bow underneath the roll; then, pulling out little strands of hair in front of Penny's ears, she rolled them around tiny brush rollers and sprayed them with hair spray. After the spray dried, she took out the rollers and pulled the coiled hair down so it formed an attractive curl along the sides of Penny's ears.

"Wow!" exclaimed Marsy. "You're a great hairdresser."

"Yeah," agreed Sheryl. "But how come you don't want to do it for yourself?"

Laughing, Diane replied, "Because I don't have to go to all this trouble for a dance!"

Looking at Diane's very short Twiggy-styled pixie cut she'd just gotten this week, they all nodded their heads in agreement. Penny added, "And you are cute as a button in that style. I've been thinking about getting my hair cut a little shorter so I could wear it in a flip."

"That would suit you, Penny, but I think we'd better get dressed or we'll be late for the dance," Sheryl encouraged. "Don't want all the guys taken before we even arrive."

"I hope Randy isn't taken," said Penny, pulling on her red plaid kilt and soft wool turtleneck sweater. "He asked me to go to the dance with him, but I told him I didn't think my parents were ready for that yet. Maybe we could have a dance or two though."

"You don't ever want to go to a dance with Randy!" Diane asserted. "He gets horny really fast."

Eyebrows pulled together, Penny looked at Diane and questioned, "What does that mean? Does he break out in warts or something?"

The other three burst into laughter. "Oh, Penny, sometimes you are so naïve," Sheryl said, patting her friend on the shoulder. Diane then explained that when one was dancing with Randy in a waltz, he would pull you close, and you could feel his private parts firm up quickly.

"Oh no! Guess I don't know anything about guys, and I don't have older brothers or sisters to clue me in. How did you know what the word meant, Sheryl? Did you dance with him?"

Sheryl shook her head. "No," she said, "but I've overhead some of the conversations J.D. and Billy have had. Enough of this; let's get going."

When they entered the gym, they were surprised to see Roger and Bernie and two of their friends on the stage wearing mop top wigs and all dressed in baby blue blazers. They were holding guitars and pretending to be the Beatles while lip-syncing their songs. Playing along with their act, a group of girls were gathered in front of the stage, bouncing and squealing as if the guys were the real thing.

During the rest of the dance, the four girlfriends enjoyed their usual circle dancing to the fast tunes. When it became waltz time, Penny managed to avoid Randy until the last dance. As he approached her, she turned quickly and, spying Billy nearby, plunged toward him. Grabbing his hand, she said, "This is ladies' choice!" He was happy to oblige, and they snuggled together and waltzed to "Unchained Melody."

Later that night, he drove the four girls to Sheryl's house even though it was only a block away. It was midnight, and he always wanted to protect his cousin and her friends from uncomfortable situations.

* * *

The rest of the semester went quickly, and soon they were on Christmas break. The Leighs, Stevenses, and Ryans spent Christmas Day together.

Between the two seasonal holidays, Sheryl and Penny often spent time at the rink skating. One day, Billy happened to be there, too. Noticing that Penny just glided around the corners, he decided to teach her how to do crossovers. He put his right arm around her waist and held her left hand in his across his chest. When they'd come to a corner of the ice, he'd pull Penny's body closer to him to give her support as he encouraged her to glide on her left foot while crossing her right one over and landing on it to make the curve.

Alma and Nora were on refreshment-stand duty for the Royal Purple that day. Watching Billy and Penny skating close together, Nora sucked in her breath and grumbled, "I don't like this."

"Oh, for heaven's sake, Nora," stated Alma. "Billy's just showing her how to do crossovers. Quit your worrying. She's just like Sheryl to him. He treats her like a cousin. Besides, he'll soon be off to college."

Meanwhile, Sheryl was observing Billy and Penny, and she had a different perspective. She later said to Penny, "I think my cousin likes you a lot. Maybe someday you'll be my cousin, too."

Soon it was New Year's Eve and there was a dance at the Legion Hall, which had been built that summer in honour of the World War II veterans. Will and Ed were members of the Legion. The new building had taken over the public dances, which used to be held at the Town Hall. The Leighs, Stevenses, and Ryans were all attending the New Year's Eve dance, including the kids. The band was the Walker family, who had played at the Town Hall dances back when Will and Ed had gone to them in their youth. Although many of the original band members were getting up in age, they were still adept, and they included the younger members of the family so eventually they could take over.

Soon after Penny and Sheryl arrived, they spotted Bernie and Roger just as the band struck up a tune for doing a Scottish Schottische. They ran over to them, grabbing their hands and saying, "Come on, guys. This is perfect for us four!" They immediately formed a square with two in front and two behind, all holding hands. Following the music's rhythm, they did the movements of the dance that they'd learned from their parents.

The next tune was appropriate for a Butterfly, which required three dance partners. Billy had just arrived, so the girls each grabbed one of his arms and linked theirs with his at the elbow. They coordinated the movements of their feet, then took turns whirling in circles with Billy, arms linked at the elbow. At the end of this dance, the Walker family started up with "Roll Out the Barrel."

"Oh, Billy, do you know how to polka?" Penny asked. "Mum just taught me in the kitchen the other night while making supper." She looked up eagerly into Billy's blue eyes.

"No, I don't, Penny. I'd stumble all over you."

"It's easy. It's just like an old-time waltz where you count one-two-three, one-two-three, but we have to do it faster and kind of hop the steps. Let's try it before the music quits."

While they were practicing the dance to Penny's counting, Ed and Will were watching them from a corner, while drinking a rum and Coke. "Our kids seem to get along pretty well," said Will.

"Yeah. They'd make a cute couple," agreed Ed. "Too bad Billy will be going off to college next year."

"He's a good guy, but I guess he's a little old for Penny."

"Like you were for Maudie?" Ed teased.

"Okay, you got me. But we were both older at that time than our kids are now, so the difference wasn't so noticeable."

"True," Ed agreed, "but they'll grow up, too."

Will nodded in the affirmative, but said, "I guess time will tell. It always does."

* * *

The rest of the school year passed quickly, and school would soon be over for the summer at the end of June. The seniors wouldn't really know if they'd passed the twelfth grade until they got the results of the provincial exams. Every high school student had to write provincial final exams in each subject at the end of the school year. These exams were a challenge because they were set by anonymous teachers within the province, so if a student's teacher hadn't happened to stress things the exam teacher did in the exam, the student could be out of luck. In addition, the students' own teachers did not grade the exams. The exams were sent in to the provincial office, and a group of anonymous teachers from the province were brought to a central place early in the summer to grade the papers. The results were then sent to the students. If they passed all the exams, they passed the grade. If they failed any subject, they would have to go to summer school or study by themselves and retake a newly created exam.

Billy was pretty sure he'd done okay and would be heading off to Assiniboine Community College in the fall. He and Penny attended the spring formal, last dance of the school year, to celebrate the graduating class. As he held Penny close while dancing to "Let It Be Me," they both wanted to be the one for each other.

Penny and Sheryl had been looking forward to spending time together during the summer at the Leighs' lake cabin, but it turned out that Sheryl wasn't going to be around much. The choir director, recognizing her special talent, had encouraged Sheryl to attend the International Music Camp at the Peace Garden.

The day she was to register, Billy and Penny drove her to the camp. The International Peace Garden was located along the United States–Canadian Border at the 49th parallel, with hundreds of acres on each side donated by the province of Manitoba and the state of North Dakota. The entrance to the Garden was west of the border customs ports of both countries, just north of Dunseith, North Dakota, and south of Boissevain, Manitoba. The Peace Garden was centrally located on the international boundary halfway from sea to sea. It was established after the First World War and dedicated in July 1932 to celebrate and symbolize the friendship and support between the two neighbouring countries. It continued to expand and develop over the following decades. Two of those developments included the International Music Camp and the Legion Athletic Camp.

As Billy approached the border south of Boissevain, he bypassed the Canadian customs and drove into the Peace Garden entrance. "Wait!" Penny shouted out. "You'll get us into trouble if you don't stop at the customs."

Billy shook his head, grinning to himself while Sheryl explained, "No, Penny. We are not entering a country. We are entering an international garden. Visitors from both sides can enter and drive around the gardens on both sides of the border. Now, when you and Billy leave the Peace Garden later today, you will have to go through the Canadian customs because you'll be entering back into our country. If all of a sudden you decided to go down into North Dakota, then you'd go through the US customs. Have you never been to the Peace Garden?"

"No, I haven't," confirmed Penny. "This is amazing!" she added, admiring the landscaping after they'd passed through the check-in point.

"After we drop off Sheryl, we'll walk up the center of the Garden and look at the mass of flowers, reflective pools, and fountains, and maybe have a bite to eat at the hotdog stand," said

Billy as he turned the car south on a winding road. "The music camp is on the US side," he explained.

"How can you go to it, Sheryl? You're a Canadian!" Penny asked.

"Penny, it's an international camp, so students from both sides can attend," explained Sheryl, stressing the word *international*. "The American students have already been here for a few weeks because they get out of school at the end of May."

"Guess I've got a lot to learn today."

"Yep. And sometime maybe you can come to the camp with me. I think they have a section for artists."

At that point, Billy pulled into the parking lot of the camp and got Sheryl's suitcase and bookbag out of the car. He and Penny waited for Sheryl to register, then after giving her hugs and wishing her their best, they watched the counselor lead her to the dorm.

As he'd promised, Billy took Penny for a walk up the center of the Peace Garden along the cement walk with steps into different levels. Beautiful flower gardens adorned both sides along the walkway, interspersed with fountains. Years later, towers and a chapel would be built at the top of the walkway with many quotes engraved on the walls from famous people from both countries.

After their walk, Billy and Penny stood on a large patio, leaning over the railing and looking into the pond below and up to the top of the walkway from which they'd just returned. "How gorgeous!" Penny exclaimed.

"Yeah," Bill agreed. "It would be a great place for a wedding." Seeing the questioning frown on Penny's face, he added, "At least, I hear a lot of folks are booking it for their special day. Anyway, let's go grab a bite to eat and head back home."

Before they left the Garden, Billy and Penny stood before the cairn situated right on the border with each country's flag on the appropriate side. Engraved on the monument from the 1932 dedication were the following words: "To God in His Glory, we two nations dedicate this garden and pledge ourselves that as long as men shall live, we will not take up arms against one another."

* * *

Sheryl was so taken with all she was learning and experiencing at the camp that she extended her sessions for all of July. Meanwhile, Billy did go to work for Will and learned a lot about mechanics in preparation for college in September. Penny took a babysitting course through the CGIT organization at the United Church and was able to make some spending money babysitting for neighbours with young children. She loved kids, and they loved her.

Occasionally on a Friday night, Billy and Penny would take in a movie at the Moonlight Drive-In. On Saturday nights, Crocus Plains was abuzz with activity. All the shops were open, and the farm families came to town to shop and visit with neighbours who had also come to town for the evening. The children often went to a movie at the Rainbow Theatre while their parents went to the Legion for a drink with friends. Some men hung out at the pub, but women weren't allowed, so wives either shopped or met friends at Wing Ling's Wok for coffee.

The teenagers cruised Central Avenue from the grain elevator at the end of the shopping center to the lake at the other end and back again. They put in time listening to their eight-track tapes of Neil Diamond and Roy Orbison while waiting for the dance to start at the lakeside pavilion. These teenagers included Billy and Penny. The excuse was that Penny couldn't drive yet, so Billy offered to take her. The truth of the matter was that they were spending a lot of time together, much to Nora's displeasure. Penny did upon occasion have a dance or two with Roger and Bernie, but most everyone at the dance considered her and Billy a couple, as they always had the last dance together. It was their Friday nights at the drive-in, however, that confirmed their closeness. Toward the end of the summer, Billy began pulling Penny onto his side of the car, keeping his arm snug around her waist. Turning her face toward his and brushing his lips across hers soon turned into a natural habit of kissing.

When Sheryl finally got home for the last couple of weeks of August, Penny thought they would finally have time together, and she was anxious to share her feelings for Billy with his cousin. As it happened, the Leighs were soon off to Minnedosa to attend J.D.'s wedding to Stella, whom he'd met at college. Sheryl was singing at the wedding. The Ryans had been invited, but they were making a trip to London to visit Maudie's brothers, Penny's uncles John and Larry. It wasn't until after Labour Day when school started again that the best friends were able to be together. Billy, of course, was off to Assiniboine Community College in Brandon. He often came home on weekends under the auspices of working with Will, but he mainly came to see Penny.

Meanwhile during the school year, Sheryl and Penny continued to have fun with Diane and Marsy and, of course, Bernie and Roger, following them in their sports. In return, their friends supported their activities, too. The school had decided to put on the musical *Calamity Jane*. Sheryl's experience at the music camp had pushed her talent beyond that of the others in the school, and she got the lead role. Mr. Benson, who still supervised the art club, took charge of building and painting the set. Boys like Bernie and Roger from the Industrial Arts class helped with the construction, and Penny and others from the art club painted the scenery.

What touched Penny most about the production was the song "Secret Love," which had become a popular radio hit by Doris Day. As she listened to Sheryl sing it, Penny would finger the chain around her neck that carried Billy's birthstone ring, which he had given her that summer as a promise of their future. The ring at the end of the chain was kept hidden underneath her blouse next to her bosom. Most girls who'd been given rings by their boyfriends wrapped yarn or tape around the band so it would fit their ring finger, wearing it proudly for all to see. Billy, on the other hand, was Penny's "secret love."

* * *

The high school years and summers passed much like those first ones, and soon the girls were looking forward to their own graduation. They'd both decided to go to Brandon University to prepare to become high school teachers, Sheryl in English and Penny in math.

One day after school, Sheryl said, "Penny, can you come for a Coke at the Crocus Cafe with me? I have something to share with you."

"Sure," replied Penny, wondering about Sheryl's serious tone. "It's not bad news, is it?"

"No. But it's not exactly what we were expecting or planning."

After they got settled into a booth with their Cokes and chips, Penny, unable to wait any longer, said, "Okay, spill it!"

Sheryl handed her an envelope from the University of North Dakota and told her to read the letter inside.

Penny's face changed expressions several times as she read the letter. Sheryl had been offered a scholarship to the university to major in English with the possibility of being a part of the Concert Choir. "Wow! How did this happen? What are you going to do?"

"One of the instructors at the International Music Camp I attended each summer was from Grand Forks, North Dakota, and he has connections to the university. He got me to apply for admission, and when I was accepted, he was able to get this offer for me. I really didn't have any intentions of going; I just applied because he wanted me to. Now what am I going to do? I'm so torn. It's a fantastic opportunity, but I don't want to give up our university years together." A teardrop trickled down her cheek.

Penny reached out and patted Sheryl's hand. "I get your dilemma, and of course I wanted you as my roommate for the next four years, but this truly is an exceptional opportunity, and you can't give it up. Just think, kiddo, with your talent and the prospects this might bring, you might end up on Broadway!"

They both chuckled at that, but Penny continued, "Really, girl, you can't give this up. This chance may open many doors for you. It's kind of like our Canadian hockey boys going down there as a potential road to the NHL. I'd never forgive myself or you if you gave this up just for me."

"You really are the best friend ever, Penny. Thank you for your understanding."

Little did they know this would not be the last serious talk they'd have before they both went off to university. It was 1967, Canada's Centennial, so before any further serious discussions arose, they spent much of that summer participating in celebration activities until the last couple of weeks before starting the next chapter of their lives.

Chapter
FOURTEEN

"What am I going to do? I have to stop this! It's gone on too long. It's getting too serious, and she's eighteen now. She's an adult. She will do what she wants to do, and no one can stop her. How did I let this happen?" Nora cried out to her sister, bursting into tears.

Alma put her arm around Nora, trying to comfort her. "Maybe nothing will happen. Penny is going off to Brandon University. Billy is done at Assiniboine Community College and is going off to join the military. He's following in J.D.'s footsteps. So he won't be in Brandon anymore."

"But don't you see? She's eighteen. He could ask her to marry him, or worse, just live with him."

"Have you considered talking to Maudie? She'd probably agree with you."

"I couldn't tell her all the reasons I don't want them to be together. She'd figure it had something to do with my not liking her because she married my best friend Grace's husband. Can you imagine her reaction if I gave her more details? I can just hear her English accent saying, 'What the bloody hell?'"

"Well, you may have a point. You know, maybe Sheryl could talk to Penny. They're having a girls' weekend at our cabin together this weekend. It's their last chance before they go their separate ways to university."

Shocked, Nora yelled at Alma, "You told Sheryl?!"

"Of course not, Nora. I'll have to explain everything to her with some cautions as to how she approaches the subject."

Nora sighed. "I guess I have no other choice. But one of the cautions must be that neither she nor Penny must ever tell anyone else." She added a few specifics, then cried again in her sister's arms.

* * *

Two nights later, Sheryl and Penny sat on the double porch swing, which had been moved to the deck of the Leighs' lake cottage. It was a lovely fall evening, and it had cooled off enough so that the girls were relaxing with some hot chocolate. They watched the beautiful sunset go down across the lake, the sun glowing through the colourful scenery set by the turning leaves on the trees.

Sheryl had been quieter than usual. *How am I going to start this story?* Finally, she took a sip of her hot chocolate, sucked in her breath, and asked, "Have you and Billy ever done it?"

Penny looked quizzically at Sheryl. "Done what? What are you talking about?"

Sheryl heaved a sigh and said, "Oh, come on Penny. You know what I mean. Did you ever get it on, go to bed together, sleep together, have intercourse? Oh, Penny, don't make me go on. You know. Have you ever had sex?"

Penny had started snickering watching Sheryl run through her repertoire. She said, "I can't believe you asked me that! Why do you need to know? And no, we haven't. Not that we haven't wanted to, and we've come close, but we didn't want to risk getting pregnant, especially when I was still in high school."

"Thank God!" Sheryl exclaimed, heaving another sigh, this time of relief.

Penny looked at her, frowning. "Why is it important to you? Why should you care? And is it really any of your business?"

"Well, Penny, it is my business, because you're my best friend and Billy's my cousin. I'm afraid I have something to share with you. You can't be intimate with Billy, and you can't ever marry. In fact, you need to break up with him. He's your half brother."

"What? That can't be! It's impossible! Have you lost your mind?"

"No, Penny. I wish I had."

Sheryl then went on to tell Nora's story. After Will had lost Grace in childbirth, he'd been devastated. Nora had been Grace's best friend. While they were at her graveside together, Nora had invited Will for supper so they weren't alone and so they could comfort one another in their loss. Nora was also worried about losing Ed, who was training with the Winnipeg Rifles and would soon be shipped overseas to the European theatre of World War II. Will had missed Ed also because they were best friends, and he had felt bad that he hadn't signed up with Ed. He and Nora had both needed comfort, which had turned into a sudden physical connection that helped them momentarily escape their sorrows.

Will had regretted betraying his friend. Feeling he couldn't stay in Crocus Plains where he'd be constantly reminded of his lost love and the betrayal of his friend, he immediately signed up with the Winnipeg Rifles and was able to join Ed on their journey through the war.

After having intercourse with Will, Nora had missed her period, and experiencing other symptoms, she soon realized she must be pregnant. Since she'd had her period shortly after Ed had left for the military, she knew the baby couldn't be his; it had to be Will's.

After giving Penny the story, Sheryl continued with Nora's restrictions. "You have to break up with Billy, Penny, but you can never tell him why. Nora doesn't want his relationship with

Ed, the father who raised him, to be destroyed. He already has a closeness to Will that may have been a natural connection. Will and Ed must also never know; it would ruin their friendship, and Nora's afraid it might also end her marriage. She couldn't stand to lose both her son and her husband."

"This is too much to take in. I love Billy. How can I break up with him?" Penny asked, her head buried in her hands.

Patting her back, Sheryl suggested, "Maybe your love is natural like his connection to your dad. You're siblings. You're clever, Penny. You'll think of some way to make this separation logical. I'm sorry I can't be around for you, Penny, but I have to leave for UND tomorrow. University is starting earlier in North Dakota than in Brandon."

"I guess I can't even share this with Mum. It would kill her. No wonder Nora was always a little cool with her. Mum attracted and married Dad, Nora's lover and the father of her son."

* * *

The following week tore Penny apart. She couldn't look at her mother or her dad without choking up. And when she ran into Nora on the sidewalk outside Foster's Foods, all she could do was scowl at her.

It became clear to her now why Billy did not have the hair and eye colouring of his parents. She had learned in biology that brown eyes are the dominant colour and that they can reproduce a baby with blue eyes. She'd thought that had been the explanation. Now she knew the real reason was the genetics he'd gotten from her dad, who had fair hair and blue eyes.

There were only four days left before the Labour Day weekend. Penny had to leave for Brandon University on Monday. While she packed her clothes, toiletries, and school supplies, she wracked her brain, trying to decide what she was going to say to

Billy. He was coming home that weekend before his first posting at CFB Borden in Ontario. He was hoping to be assigned at some point to a foreign country like Turkey.

Before she knew it, it was Friday night and Billy was at the Ryans' front door. Opening the door, Will shook Billy's hand and patted him firmly on the back, saying, "Welcome home, son. It's great to see you. Come on in. Let's go to the kitchen and see Maudie. Penny will be out in a few minutes."

Standing in the hallway outside her bedroom, Penny cringed at the word "son" her father had used for Billy. Choking, she said to herself, "He doesn't even know he really is his son."

Pulling herself together with difficulty, Penny made her way to the kitchen, where she found her mother hugging Billy, welcoming him back. After the hug, Bill turned away from Maudie and saw Penny. He immediately strode toward her and pulled her into his arms, kissing her deeply. Maudie and Will looked at one another, grinning at this young love. "Hey, you two," interrupted Maudie, "how about you save that until we've had some supper."

Pulling away from Billy, Penny said, "No, Mum, we need some time to talk. Let's go, Billy, and take a ride down to the lake. We can always pick up something at one of the places down there."

"Penny, you've got all weekend. Stay here for supper. I've prepared Billy's favourites."

Ignoring her mother and grabbing Billy's hand, Penny pulled him with her toward the front door, thinking that there was less time than any of them might think.

Billy was pleased that Penny was so urgent in her desire to spend time alone. He drove them down to the beach, parked the car, and asked, "Want to go over to the Dairy Queen for a bite to eat?"

"Not yet, Billy. We have to talk. Let's walk through the park."

Looking at her, his eyebrows pulled together in confusion, he said, "Okay, let's go. What's up?"

As they walked through the colourful oak trees, acorns pelting the ground around them, Penny swallowed hard and began her approach to separation. "Don't you think, Bill, that we have kind of started down separate paths in our lives?"

"What do you mean? I think we have always been on the same path, and it was meant to be. We've been close ever since we were kids."

"Yes," Penny agreed. "It was almost like we were related when we were little. Like we were all a part of the same family. Our families, including Sheryl's, spent a lot of time together."

"True, but you and I became more than being like cousins or siblings. Penny, you're the love of my life."

"I love you, too, Billy, but I don't think we're meant to be together. We have different goals. You want to have a military life like your cousin J.D. and travel all over the world. I want to pursue teaching, so I have four years of schooling yet. During that time, we're going to be far from one another, and we'll probably grow apart. After I'm finished with my degree and teacher preparation, I'll want to find a position in a school here on the prairies, maybe even in Crocus Plains. I wouldn't be able to use my education if we're travelling all over the country and world."

"Oh, but there are other things for you to do. We can get married sooner rather than later and have a family. Being a mum would be a really important job."

"You don't get it, Billy," Penny replied firmly. "You're three years older than I am. You've been able to follow your dreams and desires. I think I should be able to find myself, too, before committing to family life."

"Are you sure, Penny? This doesn't sound like you. You've changed," Billy said, frowning at her in disbelief.

"That's exactly what I'm saying, Bill. We've both changed. Neither of us are the people we used to be. I grew up."

"Are you saying it's over, Penny?"

"I guess I am, Bill."

"The fact that you're calling me Bill rather than Billy is telling me something. Guess I'd better get you home now."

There was no discussion as they walked back to the car and drove to the Ryans' home. As he pulled up to the house, Billy said, "Well, I guess this is it. Good luck with university."

"And good luck with your military career," Penny responded as she climbed out of the car. Before she closed the door, she pulled the chain with his ring off her neck and tossed it at him.

While closing the door, she saw a silly grimace on his face as he said, "A penny for your thoughts." With that, he drove away.

If he only knew my real thoughts. They're worth more than a penny. I'm dying inside. Trying hard to hold back tears, Penny slipped quietly through the front door and made it to her room before her parents realized she was back home. Curling up in the fetal position, she silently cried herself to sleep.

CHAPTER
FIFTEEN

W aking the next morning, Penny realized she was completely alone. Billy was no longer in her life, and she had no one to talk to about the conundrum in which she was now living. She couldn't talk to her parents, and Sheryl was already at the University of North Dakota. Penny feared running into Nora lest Penny unleashed her frustrations with Nora and vice versa. It was a good thing she was leaving town the next day for Brandon University. Perhaps this new chapter in her life would be like starting over, and she could at least put the past behind even if she would never be able to forget it.

The next day, riding in the back seat of the car so she wouldn't have to be close to either of her parents, Penny wondered who her roommate would be since it was no longer Sheryl. She hoped they'd get along. At least Diane and Marsy would be staying in the Women's Residence, too. Unfortunately, their presence might bring back a flood of memories that would be hard to handle. She hoped she'd be able to keep them from reminiscing too much.

Beginning to cough, Penny asked, "Mum, can you please open a window?" Maudie had never given up smoking, and the residue from her cigarette was wafting into the back seat to Penny.

"Sure, dear," her mother answered. Rolling the window down, she began to laugh. "This reminds me of our Sunday drives in the summer when you were little. You'd sit up front between us, and you'd keep asking me if you could sit on the side instead of the middle so you could roll the window down and stick your head out to get away from my smoke. Guess you haven't changed."

"Guess not," Penny agreed, thinking that her life certainly had, and that was bound to change her, too.

Arriving at the university, Will and Maudie helped Penny unload her suitcase and boxes to take to her room. At the front desk, she checked in with the secretary. As she was about to lead her parents to her room, a voice called out to her. Turning around, Penny was greeted by a grey-haired woman who was the Dean of the Women's Residence. Welcoming her, the dean handed Penny a packet of information about the dorm's rules and told her there would be a meeting the next evening in the downstairs TV room to go over items and answer questions.

Penny and her parents then hauled her belongings up the stairs to the second floor and down the hall to her assigned room. Just as she was unlocking the door, she heard, "Penny!" Turning to her left, she saw Diane and Marsy come out of the room next door. "Hey," Marsy cried out. "We're neighbours! Isn't that great?"

Having mixed feelings about the situation, Penny accepted her friends' hugs but cut off further conversation. "Guess I'd better get inside and get unpacked. Talk to you guys later."

"Yeah," said Diane, turning back to her and Marsy's room. "We'll knock on your door when it's time to go down for supper. Nice seeing you, Mr. and Mrs. Ryan."

After helping her get settled in, Will asked if Penny wanted to go for supper with them before they went back to Crocus Plains. "No, Will," Maudie interrupted. "You heard her friend say they'd get her for supper here in the residence. It's probably better for her to get used to the dorm living routine before classes begin."

Wondering if her mother sensed a little discomfort within her, Penny said, "Yeah, Dad. Mum's right, and you probably want to get home before it gets too late. Thanks for bringing me over and helping me get settled into my room. I'll do a few more things while I wait for my new roommate. I hope she comes today."

Her parents both hugged her and wished her their best. "Call if you need anything," Will said as he and Maudie walked down the hallway to the stairs.

Penny organized some items on the bookshelves above her desk, making room for the texts she'd have to buy once she got the syllabi from her classes. She glanced out the window, noting that to the left she could see the men's residence. At ground level were the glassed-in walkways that joined both residences to a lounge area and adjoining dining room, which she could see straight ahead from the window.

She was thinking that perhaps she had been selfish taking the desk and twin bed beside the window before her roommate arrived, when suddenly she heard a key in the door. Turning around, Penny saw a young woman walk in carrying a suitcase. She was about Penny's height and was slender with hazel eyes and a reddish-blond pixie haircut.

"Hi, I'm Penny Ryan. I guess we're roommates."

The young woman smiled and reached out her hand to shake Penny's. "Yes, we are. My name is Ginny McIntyre."

"Welcome, Ginny." Looking at the suitcase Ginny had just placed on the floor at the end of the other twin bed, Penny asked, "Is that all you have?"

"No. My brother dropped me off at the front door, unloaded my things, and took off. I'll be making a few trips downstairs to bring up the rest."

"Oh, let me help you. By the way, I took the window side, but I should have waited until you came for us to choose. If you like, we can flip a coin to see who gets it."

Ginny laughed. "No, I'm perfectly fine with this side. But I will take you up on helping me bring up the rest of my stuff."

"You got it!"

The two made a couple of trips bringing up Ginny's supplies. While she got her things organized, they shared things about their backgrounds and what they were here to study. Ginny was from Neepawa. She planned to be an English major, and she dreamed of becoming a writer like her favourite author, Margaret Laurence, who had also come from Neepawa. "But," she concluded, "I'll probably just end up teaching."

"Oh, don't give up your dream, Ginny. You might end up doing both. My best friend from high school, well, of my entire life actually, was going to study English here and become a high school teacher. This is serendipity. You were meant to be my roommate."

"Where is she? Didn't she come to university?" Ginny asked.

"Yes, she's at university, but in North Dakota. She got a scholarship to the University of North Dakota in Grand Forks. She's so talented. She can sing and act. I keep thinking she's going to be on stage someday, but she keeps telling me I'm dreaming for her."

Their conversation was interrupted by a rap on the door. It was Diane and Marsy coming to pick up Penny for supper. "This is my roommate, Ginny McIntyre, and these are two of my friends from Crocus Plains." After introducing them, she continued, "Well, let's go see what kind of grub they've got for us students."

The four girls chatted, getting to know one another as they walked downstairs and across the glassed-in walkway to the lounge area. Students were lining up to grab a tray and go through the cafeteria to get served supper and to find a table in the dining room. The line was long, and it wound around in a long snakelike U. Being toward the tail end of the line, Penny looked across to the other side of the line and spotted Bernie and Roger just as they spotted the girls. They grinned and waved at the girls, who explained who the guys were to Ginny.

After the girls had received their meals on their trays and entered the dining room, they saw Roger and Bernie standing at a table across the room, waving at them to join them. Worried about having too many memories from home surface, Penny hoped that having Ginny in the group would help to fade some of those memories, if not totally erase them.

Not only were the first few days filled with getting registered for classes, buying texts, and finding their classrooms, but just like high school, there was Freshie week, which included some hazing.

After a couple of weeks, they were all oriented and fairly comfortable in their new setting. The guys were not allowed to visit in the girls' rooms. They could only come into the front desk area of the residence and have the girls called down to visit them in a small lounge. The senior students had informed the girls that this didn't always stop the guys from attempting a raid just for fun. Sure enough, one evening about a month later they heard laughter and running down their halls, and soon there was rapping on doors. It was kind of scary, and Penny and Ginny double-checked to make sure their door was locked.

Soon there was a rap on their door and on Diane and Marsy's. "It's us!" they heard in low voices, Roger at one door and Bernie at the other. Somewhat hesitantly, the girls let them in, and then they all joined together in one room.

"How the heck did you get in?" Penny asked.

"Well," explained Roger, "the seniors said they always have an accomplice in your residence who leaves the end door ajar so the guys can sneak in. It's become sort of a tradition at the beginning of the school year."

"That's one I can do without," said Ginny. "It's kind of scary."

At that moment, one of the senior guys ran down the halls, telling all the others, "Get out—NOW!" Bernie and Roger hustled out just before the dean and the security guard walked down the hall, ready to shoo every guy out after taking down their names.

"Don't think we'll ever do that again," said Roger two nights later when the six of them were downstairs in the Commons area under the lounge and cafeteria. There was a canteen there, so they were all at a table having an evening snack of Coke and chips while visiting. Over in one corner, there was a television where a group of students were watching a hockey game.

"I was surprised you guys did it at all," said Marsy.

"Yeah," agreed Penny. "That's not like you guys at all."

"Well, Guess we were trying to fit in," explained Bernie. "It seemed like it was a little leftover hazing. But like Roger said, we won't be doing that again."

"What are you guys studying?" Ginny asked.

"I'll be majoring in math," Roger responded. "I hope someday to transfer into the engineering program at the University of Manitoba."

"I'm not sure what I'm going to do," said Bernie. "I'll probably major in history or philosophy for now. Good general subjects for folks who don't know what they're doing, if anything at all. Say, Penny, have you heard from Sheryl? How's she doing with the Yanks?"

"No, I haven't heard from her yet. I'm hoping she'll be home at Christmas so we can catch up. We better get going, gals, before we can't get into the residence. I think we already may have to get the security guard to let us in." Penny pushed her chair away from the table and gathered up her paper cup and plate to throw in the wastebasket.

"The rules really are strict," Diane agreed. "The residence is all locked up, and past ten o'clock we have to get the guard to let us in even if the curfew is later than that. There's an eleven-o'clock curfew during the week, and it's one o'clock on weekends. If we're going to be gone for the weekend, we have to sign out and sign back in when we return. They're almost worse than the rules at home were. Anyway, see you guys Friday night. They're having a sock hop down here."

When the four girls got back to their rooms, they decided to have a Ouija board night before bedtime. They sometimes did the activity as if it were a game just for fun. They'd sit on the floor around the flat board. The board had the alphabet, numbers, and some words like *yes*, *no*, and *goodbye* on it. A small piece of wood called a planchette would be placed on the board, and the girls would place their fingers together, touching it. They'd ask a question, and presumably the spirits would move the planchette to letters, numbers, or words to answer the question. It was always a little questionable whether one of the girls actually was directing the movement, but for the most part, they believed in the supernatural responses.

On this night, they were asking questions about relationships. When it was Penny's turn, she asked, "Will I ever have a true love in my life?"

The planchette immediately began to move first toward the word *yes* and then to the letters *r* and *b*.

"Who would that be?" asked Ginny.

"I don't know," responded Penny.

Marsy wondered if it stood for Roger and Bernie. "No," Penny replied emphatically. "First of all, you can't have two true loves, and second, they've been longtime friends. I'd never think of them in any other way." They all agreed and decided to call it a night.

* * *

The group had made their way through the first semester and were all back home for the Christmas holidays. Ginny, of course, went north to Neepawa. Normally the Leighs, Ryans, and Stevenses would have Christmas dinner together, but this year the excuse Nora used for them not to be all together was that Billy and Penny had broken up and she didn't want to make them uncomfortable. Will and Maudie still didn't understand what had happened between the kids, but they agreed that it was probably too soon. Billy, on the other hand, not knowing the real reason they'd broken up, tried to convince his mother to invite the Ryans, hoping seeing him again might change Penny's mind about the breakup.

Penny and Sheryl did get to spend some time together, and they shared their university experiences. Sheryl was thrilled that she'd been selected for the Concert Choir.

"After the holidays, I've been chosen to sing the national anthem at the hockey games. I'm going to have to get it memorized so I don't accidentally break into 'O Canada'!"

"Do you feel comfortable in a foreign country?" Penny asked.

"Well, North Dakota is a lot like Manitoba, and my classmates grew up on the prairies, too, but they call it the Northern Plains. I guess that's the one thing that is a bit bothersome. I'm often teased about how I pronounce words like *again* as if it would rhyme with 'pain.' And they all think I say 'aboot' instead of 'about.' I know we say it a little differently, but I've never said 'aboot' in my life!"

"That would get to you after a while, eh?" Penny said laughing, knowing "eh" was probably another tease item.

Sheryl giggled along with her, then suddenly quietened down and asked, "How are you doing, Penny? I've been thinking about you and Billy ever since our last weekend together. What did you tell him?"

Tears stinging her eyes, Penny explained, "It was rough. I basically told him we had different goals and that we seemed to be going our separate ways. He got the picture that I wanted to break up." She then began full-out sobbing. "But I didn't want to break up. I kept hoping it was all a mistake. I guess I just didn't want to face reality."

"I think Billy was hoping to see you at Christmas so that he could talk you into getting back together."

"I wish I could tell him the truth. Then he'd understand. But I promised not to. Is he doing okay?"

"Not so much personally, but he is enjoying the military. He seems to think he's found his calling. He and J.D. had a great time comparing experiences. By the way, J.D. and Stella are expecting their first child. I'm going to be an auntie."

"Oh, fun! Congratulations. I'm glad there's some happy news this holiday."

The holidays were soon over, and with the snap of a finger, the school year was over, too. Penny thought she and Sheryl would have a great summer together now that Sheryl wouldn't be going to the International Music Camp. Wrong. As it turned out, Sheryl was asked to come back as a counselor and singing instructor for the youngest students at the camp. Penny, meanwhile, continued to do some babysitting, but she also got a job as a waitress at Bakker's Beach Barbecue, a restaurant down by Jackfish Lake.

* * *

The following summers and university years passed just as quickly as the first one had, and Sheryl and Penny were soon in their final year. Degrees in the US were four years, but Sheryl's final year could also include teacher preparation. The degrees in Canada were three years, so Penny had already graduated with her math major, but now she was enrolled in a professional year of teacher preparation for certification.

Penny and Ginny still roomed together, but the organizational structure of the residence had changed considerably from their early years. There was no longer a Dean of both the women's and men's residences. They each had a Don, who was a senior student who was given the former dean's suites and meals free for the responsibility of the job. The rules and regulations were also determined by the residents, led by a president chosen from among them, who sat on the joint residence council. Ginny had been asked to take the don's position for the women's residence, now named Flora Cowan Hall after the former dean. She was allowed to share the suite with Penny, who would be her assistant and substitute for her if she was away for a weekend. Bernie, who was also in the professional certification program, had been selected for the don position in the men's residence, and he shared his suite with Roger, who was taking some extra post-degree courses to get his prerequisites for the engineering program.

The first week of the fall semester, the two residences had a gathering in the Commons area downstairs. Ginny and Bernie each gave a welcome-back speech to the new and returning students. There was music and chatting at the tables, with men and women residents mixed together at each table. The two student resident presidents had prepared a game to mix up the residents at the tables so they could get to know more students from their joint residences. There would be more events planned between the residence halls, and rules had loosened considerably so that there could be visits between men and women in their dorm rooms as long as they were signed in and out.

The canteen was open, of course, and the student running it was a friend of Bernie and Roger's. When he brought over an extra plate of treats for them, they introduced him to their female friends.

"Gals, this is our friend Tyler Jackson. He's from Dauphin. He's been living off campus during his first years, so that's why you haven't met him before," said Roger.

"We've had classes together, and he also worked up at Clear Lake during the summers like we did," added Bernie. He then went around the table, giving Tyler the girls' names.

When he came to Penny, she looked up from her hamburger into blue eyes that became mutually entranced with her brown ones. She smiled and said, "I've been thinking of picking up some part-time work to add a little spending money to my budget. I've worked in a restaurant during the summers. Do you possibly need any help?"

"Absolutely!" Tyler replied. "You can start tomorrow if you like."

As the two continued to gaze at one another, the others sitting around the table started looking at one another, eyebrows rising and heads tilting in a question. Finally, residents from the other tables started calling for Tyler's attention, so he turned and went back to the counter.

"What's going on, Penny?" asked Diane.

"Nothing. What do you mean?"

"That was some pretty interesting eye communication you had with Tyler," added Ginny.

"Oh, he just reminded me of Billy," responded Penny, wondering if that really did have anything to do with the instant attraction. Or was there such a thing as love at first sight?

"Yeah, he did look a bit like Billy with his blue eyes and sandy hair. Whatever happened between you two, anyway?" Marsy asked.

Oh shit! thought Penny. *I've avoided this conversation for three years. Why did it have to arise now?* She then answered glibly, "Oh, we just grew apart, that's all. I was just a kid when we first started seeing one another, but I grew up, and I guess I outgrew him. After all, he was almost like a brother to me."

"That's true," said Bernie, and they all nodded their heads in agreement. "Your families spent so much time together your whole lives. It was just like you were relatives."

"Exactly," agreed Penny, and then she excused herself, feigning exhaustion and the need to go to bed.

* * *

After supper the next day, Penny reported to the canteen counter in the Commons area.

"Hi there, Penny. Glad you made it. Let's take a few minutes before the guys and dolls start coming down for their evening snacks and chats to go over where everything is. We can start this first night with you taking orders, and I'll do the cooking. That will be a big help."

"Sounds like a plan, Tyler. I can get the drinks and things, too, while you're busy making the food."

"You got it, girl. I think we're going to be a good team."

The evening went well. They seemed able to read one another's minds, responding to needs and requests without being asked. When it was time to close down, Penny insisted on helping to clean up.

"Thanks for your help tonight, Penny. You're a gem. Let me walk you up to your residence," Tyler said. As they climbed the stairs to the lounge area, he took her hand and said, "I'm so glad we met."

"Me, too," she replied, not withdrawing her hand. They entered the glass walkway to Flora Cowan Hall and stood for a moment, surrounded by a few couples kissing goodnight. They were all waiting on the guard to come let them in. Again, entranced by one another's eyes, Penny thought Tyler might be going to kiss her in this romantic atmosphere, but the guard arrived at that moment to let all the women in.

She worked with Tyler every other night the following week. One evening after they'd closed up, he suggested they go for a short walk around the campus. It was dark out, but there was a beautiful fall full moon. Stopping outside Clark Hall, the main administration building, Tyler suggested they sit on the steps of the old stone building for a while. Taking her hand in his, he said, "It may be too soon to say this, but I can't help it. From the moment I met you, I've felt a deep sense of connection. Am I wrong to think that you are feeling it, too?"

"No, Tyler. You're not wrong. That first night in the Commons at the residence gathering when Bernie and Roger introduced you, I asked myself, *Is there really such a thing as love at first sight?*"

"I knew it!" he exclaimed. Putting his arm around her, he pulled her closer to his side and asked, "Is it okay then if I kiss you?"

Penny's response was to turn her face to his, put her loose hand up to his neck, and pull his head toward her so that their lips met in a passionate bond.

"I'd better get you back to the residence," Tyler said. "Don't want Ginny on my case, wondering where you are. Are you going to be able to work Saturday night?"

"Wouldn't miss it."

They parted in the lounge area, each going alone to their own entrance walkway so as not to get those sitting on the lounge couches speculating about them, even though most of them were couples engrossed in their own snuggles.

On Saturday nights the Commons was often filled because many of the residents who hadn't gone home for the weekend gathered in the corner by the television to watch *Hockey Night in Canada*. There was a sliding accordion-style panel that blocked off part of the area so the game wouldn't disturb others in the Commons who were there to snack and visit.

At the end of the game, it was also closing time, so Penny and Tyler cleaned up the concession counter and tables out front. The place was empty, so they turned off the lights, and Penny started toward the stairs.

"Why don't we go sit in the television area?" Tyler suggested. "There's a couch right behind that sliding section, and we could have some privacy to talk for a change."

"Oh, okay," Penny agreed and followed Tyler behind the panel.

They sat on the couch close together and rehashed some of the crazy things that had happened that evening. As the conversation progressed, Tyler slid his arm around Penny's shoulders, pulling her closer. As she looked toward him, he bent his head down to brush his lips across hers. Putting her arm around his neck, she snuggled closer. Eyes closed, their lips pressed firmly together, then opened to receive the dancing motions of their tongues. Tyler slid his hand up the outside of Penny's jean-covered thigh onto her waist and eventually reached her breast. He gently massaged it over her shirt, arousing a slight groan from her.

"Ahem!" said a voice, startling the two of them. Pulling away from one another and looking up, they saw the security guard staring down at them. "I wondered where you two were tonight since you hadn't come up to the lounge area to get to your residences. I won't comment on your questionable activity, but this area is off-limits for anyone after the Commons is closed at ten o'clock. So get out of here."

Embarrassed and a little scared, they both jumped up and headed for the stairs. After that night, they realized they had no place of their own for privacy, and they assumed that the passionate part of their connection would have to be put on hold. They did, however, take a drive in Tyler's car a couple of times up to the North Hill, where they found a secluded spot to make out. Ginny also went home to Neepawa one weekend, and they had the privacy of her suite for a little bit. They never went all the way, but they certainly went far enough to arouse the passion in their connection.

Before they knew it, it was Christmas, and they were both going to their own hometowns for the holiday. Waving to her as he went to his car, Tyler said, "See you in the new year. I've gotta go see my other girlfriend," then laughed. Penny looked at him at first with a question in her eyes, then laughed, too, knowing he was joking.

Will had driven into Brandon to pick Penny up and bring her home to Crocus Plains. Maudie met her at the door with open arms. "How's my baby girl?" she asked.

"Not a baby anymore, Mum."

"You'll always be my baby, even when you have babies of your own," Maudie replied. "We're going over to the Leighs this evening. Sheryl is home, too, and we parents know you two will want to get together. They will be spending most of the holidays with J.D., Stella, and their daughters, Abbey and Lucy, because they are leaving in the new year for the Queen Charlotte Islands. He's been posted there as the commanding officer. He's certainly on a roll with his career and his family, too. I don't think you knew they had a second daughter last summer."

"Wow! Thanks for letting us get together. I'm sure Sheryl and I have a lot of catching up to do."

After supper, Maudie packed up her famous fruitcake, made from her family recipe, to take to the Leighs. Will, on the other hand, brought a bottle of rum and Baileys Irish Cream. "Something for everyone," he said, grinning at Penny.

"Thanks, Dad. I'm old enough to try it. Isn't it ironic though that the year I turn twenty-one, Canada changes the drinking age to eighteen?"

After they arrived at the Leighs, the parents cozied up around the fireplace, and Sheryl said to Penny, "Let's take a glass of wine to my room so we can have a good heart to heart."

"Sounds good to me," Penny agreed. Sitting on the window seat in Sheryl's room, they sipped their wine and watched the large snowflakes floating to the ground. "So, what's been happening this final year with you?" Penny asked.

"Well, nothing much." Then grinning mischievously, Sheryl added, "I'm just in love. That's all."

"What? Me, too! You go first. Tell me all about it."

Sheryl explained that she had met a fellow Canadian at UND who was there on a hockey scholarship. "His name is Deacon Cross, and he's originally from Saskatchewan. He's handsome, a great player, and a gentleman. He's not a hockey goon. Like all guys though, Deacon has a dream of making it into the NHL."

"Wow. Is it serious between the two of you?"

"It's a little early, but I think so. Now what about your story?"

After Penny explained about her and Tyler, Sheryl commented, "That's sounding serious, too. How about your roommate, Ginny? Is she still at BU?"

Penny explained that Ginny was now the don of the residence and that Penny was allowed to share her suite as her assistant.

"You're lucky. Ginny has always sounded like a neat gal, kind of like us. I've got a new roommate this year. Her name's Tiffany, and she's a puck bunny. She hasn't a clue about the game of hockey, but she's all over the players. Sometimes I get the impression she's maybe a little jealous of me and Deacon."

"Sorry about that. Yes, I'm lucky to have a friend like Ginny. I even told her about Billy. I can trust her to keep it to herself. She actually cried when I told our story."

"Yep. She is like us. You won't have to worry about seeing Billy this holiday. Aunt Nora, Uncle Ed, and Billy are going to spend the holidays with J.D. and his family, too. Billy's always looked up to J.D. and has followed in his footsteps. I think he's being posted somewhere else soon, too. He enjoyed his first two years in Borden, Ontario, and the last two in Calgary, Alberta. I think he may have met someone there, too."

"Oh, I hope so, Sheryl. I still love him, but I think it is turning more into a platonic love, like that of a sister, and I so want him to find happiness in his life, both in work and love."

"Guess that's about it for our time this Christmas. Next time we see one another, I will have graduated, and you will be certified to teach. What are your plans, Penny?"

"Well, I have a potential job here at the Crocus Plains Collegiate in the math department, so unless something unexpected happens, that's what I'll be doing next fall. What about you, Sheryl?"

"Well, I'm not sure. A lot depends on what happens with Deacon and me."

"Good luck with that, Sheryl. I hope it all works out for you. He sounds like a good guy."

"Tyler, too. Guess we'll see you in the spring and catch up again."

Hugging one another, they wished each other their best for the holidays and whatever the new year would bring.

* * *

Back at Brandon University after the holiday, Penny made her way down to the Commons area to see Tyler. As she approached the counter, Tyler looked up, slightly startled to see her. "Oh, hi," he said without much emotion.

Penny had expected a little more affectionate greeting, but said, "Hi to you, too. How was your Christmas?"

"Interesting," he said in a noncommittal tone. "I'll tell you more later. Want to go for a ride?"

Penny grinned, thinking she knew what he was implying. "Sure. What time will you be done?"

"I'll pick you up about ten o'clock."

"Okay. I'll be ready," she said enthusiastically, walking away smiling to herself.

A couple of hours later, Tyler was in his car parked in the street outside the women's residence, honking the horn. The don's window faced the street, so Penny saw who it was, donned her parka, and said to Ginny, "See you later."

"Have fun," Ginny said with a knowing smile on her face.

After Penny got in the passenger side, Tyler immediately headed for the North Hill in silence. Penny figured he was just in a hurry to get there.

After he parked in their usual secluded spot, Penny started to edge over toward his side of the car. Tyler held up his hand and said, "We have to talk."

"It sounds serious," Penny responded, hoping it was a happy seriousness.

"I guess it is serious. I'm sorry Penny, but I'm engaged."

Her eyebrows pulled together, her mouth closed, her chin dropped, and her whole face fell into a frown.

Tyler looked at her and, half smiling, said, "Well, what have you got to say? A penny for your thoughts."

She finally got her voice back and said, "How can you make jokes? What do you mean, you're engaged?"

"I'm sorry, Penny. It's not funny. Connie and I have gone together since grade eight. Remember when I said I was going to see my other girlfriend? I was only half joking. When I met you, Penny, it was an instant attraction. You are the only woman who could ever have taken me away from Connie. Over the holidays though, we spent a lot of time together, and I realized that

I couldn't give up the love I've had for a lifetime, so I asked her to marry me. I am truly so sorry."

"There's not much I can say to this but take me back to the dorm."

* * *

The university year ended in April. Both Penny and Ginny had completed their high school teacher certification program and had applied to the Manitoba Department of Education for their teaching certificates. Penny was going to her hometown school in Crocus Plains to teach math. Ginny had decided to go on for her Master's in English and was going to spend the summer in her hometown of Neepawa researching the life of Margaret Laurence, whom she planned to use as her thesis subject.

They wished one another their best as they packed up to leave for home and promised to keep in touch, recognizing that life often distracts from such promises. They both also hoped that each other would find the love of her life. Ginny had been kind of attracted to Bernie and Roger, but just like with Penny, Sheryl, Diane, and Marsy, they were just really good friends. They were both almost like one of the girls.

Penny arrived back at Crocus Plains before Sheryl because her year didn't end until the end of May. Penny always found it interesting that the Canadian school year went a month longer than that of the US, yet the Canadian university year ended a month before that of the US. Because her degree was a four-year program, Sheryl also would be going through graduation before she came home.

Toward the end of May, Penny ran into J.D. downtown. "Hi there, J.D. What are you doing back here? Are you and your family back for a visit?"

"No," J.D. sighed. "I came back for Sheryl's graduation but left Stella and the girls on the islands. I'm making a quick trip to Grand Forks tomorrow to bring Sheryl home. Dad had a heart attack yesterday. He's in Intensive Care right now. He seems to be doing okay, but we thought Sheryl would want to see him just in case. . . ."

"Oh, J.D., I'm so sorry. Is there something I can do? Should I stay with your mum while you go down to North Dakota? She must be beside herself."

"Thanks, Penny, for your offer, but it's okay. Aunt Nora is with her. I'd better get back to the house. I just came down to the bank for Mum. See you later."

Penny did see Sheryl briefly one day during the six she was in town. Sheryl hugged her sympathetically when Penny told her what had happened between her and Tyler. "How about you and Deacon?" Penny asked.

"Things are going well. In fact, he wants us to make plans to be together when I get back. He's in Rochester, New York, right now with the Americans, the Canucks' farm team. He was drafted by the Canucks while he played at UND. So I'm not sure what my future holds. What about yours?"

"Well, I did get a job teaching math at the collegiate, so I'll be here for your folks if they need some help."

"Thanks, Penny. It looks like Dad will be coming home tomorrow. He's had a good recovery, but he has to watch his health now and change some of his habits. I'm going to take the folks' car back to Grand Forks for my graduation and to pack up my things for the summer at least so I can be here for the folks. J.D. will have to get back to the Charlottes. I'll let you know what's up when I get back."

* * *

A month later, Penny and Sheryl were sitting on the deck out at the Leighs' cottage. John Leigh's health had improved so much, he was back at work in his drugstore. "I'm surprised to still see you here," Penny commented. "I thought you and Deacon were making plans for your future."

Looking at her best friend with sad eyes, Sheryl told her that when she had gotten back to UND, a letter she'd sent him explaining about her dad had been returned. "He's no longer in Rochester, but I don't know where he is. I thought he was going to call me, but Tiffany said there'd been no calls. She keeps telling me that he's a big star and that he'll have lots of females after him, so why would he stick with someone who wouldn't put out like me. Even though we've done everything but consummate our union, I'm beginning to think she may be right."

"That doesn't sound like the Deacon you described to me," Penny said, trying to assure Sheryl.

"I didn't think so either. But maybe I'm too naïve like Tiff says. Anyway, I'd better start looking for a job. I can't be dependent on the folks all my life. I hope I can get something close to Crocus Plains in case they need me at some point again."

"Hey, I know just the job," Penny exclaimed. "Katie Johanson, one of the English teachers, just requested maternity leave for the year. I'll set you up for an interview to fill in for her."

"Oh, Penny, that would be great. We would be back together again."

Sheryl got the position. At her parents' urging, she flew out to the Queen Charlotte Islands before the school year started to visit J.D., Stella, and her little nieces.

CHAPTER
SIXTEEN

*I*t was the Labour Day weekend, and Penny and Sheryl were in the collegiate getting their rooms ready for the first day of classes on Tuesday.

Taking a coffee break in the teachers' lounge, they talked about beginning their careers back where they'd made many memories together in their teens. "By the way," Sheryl asked, "where are our school-days chums Roger and Bernie? I haven't seen them all summer. They graduated from BU, too, didn't they?"

"Yeah, they did. But you know what loyal, patriotic, good guys they are. They felt they should support our neighbors to the south now that they're in the Vietnam War by signing up with the US military."

"Oh my! That does sound like them. I hope they'll be safe."

"Yeah," agreed Penny. "It's kind of ironic. Canada chose not to join the US in this confrontation, yet our Canadian boys are signing up to help out, while the American boys who disagree with the war are draft dodging into Canada. We do need to pray for our friends' safety, as well as for the safety of all the soldiers over there. It sounds like a vicious war without anyone even being sure who the enemies are or why the US is even involved."

Shaking her head in dismay, Sheryl said, "Well, I guess we'd better get back to work so we're ready to prepare the future generation."

* * *

The school year began, and soon both Sheryl and Penny had become effective, popular teachers.

One day in October, Sheryl heard from Tiffany, her former roommate at UND, asking her to be her maid of honor at her New Year's Eve wedding. She was marrying Rob Black, Deacon's buddy and former UND hockey teammate. With mixed feelings about returning to UND, where she'd lost her love, Sheryl agreed to come.

On the last day of school before the holidays, Penny was tidying up her classroom after the students had all left, excited about Christmas break. Suddenly she felt a hand on her shoulder. Turning around, she saw Peter Benson, who had been her homeroom math teacher and art club supervisor when she was a student. He now was not only the head of the math department but was also the assistant to the principal. Without warning, Mr. Benson grabbed her and kissed her.

Shocked, Penny asked, "What was that for?"

"You've always been special to me, Penny, even when you were sixteen. Now you've grown into a beautiful woman."

Not quite knowing how to handle this, she pulled away and said, "I have to get home. My mother needs me," then immediately left the room.

She met Sheryl in the hall. Noticing Penny's frowning face, Sheryl asked, "What's the matter, Penny?"

Not wanting to get into it, she used the same excuse that she had to get home to her parents to help prepare for the Christmas party they were planning.

Just before New Year's Eve, Sheryl drove down to Grand Forks for Tiffany and Rob's wedding. While there, she asked Rob about Deacon. Rob told her that Deacon was moving up from the minors to play with the Vancouver Canucks in January and was surprised she hadn't heard from him. Tiffany was a beautiful bride, and she seemed to be truly in love with Rob. He was certainly beyond head over heels in love with Tiff.

Soon after she returned home, Sheryl's dad had another heart attack. He had succumbed to his former lifestyle, drinking and eating too much of all the wrong, unhealthy things. This episode was a minor one, but it wasn't the only one during the rest of the school year.

When school began again in January, Penny found herself alone in the teachers' lounge with Mr. Benson when she was on a break. "How was Christmas, sweetie?" he asked. Before she could answer, he added, "I think we need a Happy New Year greeting," and started chasing her around the lounge. She managed to escape into the hallway and down to the library, where she pretended to look for a book, knowing that he would not follow her into this public area.

When she scanned the room, she suddenly saw Cal, Benson's son. How could he possibly be acting like such an ass when his own son was a student here? She had also heard that his poor wife had Parkinson's disease. That truly made him an asshole.

Sheryl kept asking her what the matter was, but Penny avoided talking about it. She didn't want to get Sheryl involved, and this was in the era long before women could report such situations. It would just be viewed as "some men are just like that," as her mother Maudie had once told her.

Penny had moved into the little house that the Ryans had originally lived in before her grandparents had passed away and they had taken over their larger home across the street. Will hadn't sold the little white lapsided house, and Penny had moved into it, thinking she needed to become more independent as an adult. She questioned this decision when one evening later in the spring she got a phone call. It was Benson. He wanted to pick her up and take her for a car ride on this beautiful evening. When she didn't agree right away, he then tried to bribe her. "If you come, I have some secret news about your friend Sheryl to share with you. I think the principal is a little upset with her."

Penny was sure this was an absolute lie and just a bribe to get her to come. How could she get out of this? Finally, she resorted to the old excuse every woman uses when she doesn't want to do something. "No, I can't. I have to wash my hair tonight. Goodbye."

After hanging up, she told herself she would have to let him know he had to get off her back, literally, or she would have to speak to the principal or the school board about him. Even though she knew she wouldn't do that, she thought perhaps the threat would keep him away. She was smart enough to always get herself out of an uncomfortable situation, and she didn't want his family to be disgraced by reporting him, but she had to let him know enough was enough.

While Penny was dealing with this personal issue, Sheryl was dealing with concerns about her parents. Unlike Penny, she remained in their family home to be there for them if needed. Sure enough, toward the end of the year, her dad succumbed to his unhealthy lifestyle and had a massive coronary from which he didn't recover. Her mother, Alma, went to pieces, and Sheryl worried that she might not survive this loss.

J.D. came back briefly to help take care of some business, including closing down the pharmacy and advertising its availability for sale. Sheryl had made the decision that she needed to stay by her mother for at least a year, and she was relieved when she learned Katie Johanson was returning to her position after her maternity leave that another English position had opened up. The principal was also glad to have Sheryl on staff because she could help start a glee club.

And thus began the girls' second year in their teaching careers. Penny had made it clear to Benson to leave her alone, and he eventually started looking for another position, perhaps as principal in another town. His son had graduated, and his wife needed more care than was available in town if she were to survive the Parkinson's at all. He got a vice principal's position in a large school in Winnipeg, so he was well out of the area and Penny's life. She was sure that in such a setting, he would not get away with any of his nonsense—at least she hoped not. Maybe it had been just something about her that he was attracted to over the years.

Penny started assisting Principal Bradley in many of the areas Donald Benson had, but he told her she actually did a better job than Benson had and that she might consider taking some courses in administration someday. "But right now," he said, "I need you to head up the math department. You've brought some more current ideas and methods to the students. I like the fact that you want them to understand why they do a mathematical operation, not just memorize a formula to use. I also remember your involvement with the art club as a student, and Sheryl reminded me of your work on the set for *Calamity Jane* back in the day. If she gets a musical going, perhaps you could get a group of students interested in providing the set. Glad you came back to us, Penny—or I should say Ms. Ryan."

"Thanks, Principal Bradley. I'm at your service," Penny replied. How great it was to feel so appreciated! It gave her inspiration to do even more.

They were on Easter break when Penny got an urgent call from Sheryl. "It's Mum, Penny. I just took her to the hospital. She apparently had a stroke, and I'm not sure she's going to survive."

Penny could hear the hidden tears choking Sheryl's voice. "I'll be right there, and I'll call my folks, too. Does your Aunt Nora know?"

"No, I haven't even had a chance to call J.D."

Not wanting to call Nora herself, Penny said, "I'll get Mum to call Nora, and I can call J.D. if you like."

"Thanks, Penny. I'd better talk to J.D. myself and give him the whole story. He really needs to get back here."

And he did. The next day he was able to get the needed flights off the islands and across the western provinces to Manitoba. Both he and Sheryl were sitting by their mother with Aunt Nora standing behind them when Alma said goodbye to the world. Sheryl and J.D. looked at one another, and Sheryl said, "It may have been a stroke, but I think she really died of a broken heart." J.D. nodded his head in agreement as he hugged his little sister.

Nora added, "Well, she's with John now. She will have found peace in a better place."

After the funeral, brother and sister discussed what should be done next. "You might as well keep the house for the time being, Sheryl. You need a place to stay, and there's no hurry to get rid of it. That will give you some time to go through their things, too. There may be a young pharmacist interested in the drugstore, but he said he needed to look into a few things first, financing its purchase for one thing."

"Sounds good, J.D. Thanks for taking care of things. I'll certainly keep the house until at least the end of the school year and go through their things as you suggested. I'm not sure, though, what my future plans will be. I really have no reason now to stay in Crocus Plains. With everything that's happened over the last couple of years, I think it's time that I reassess my life and my goals."

Recognizing that the pain of losing Deacon also played a role in her ambiguity toward her future, J.D put his arm around her and said, "Whatever works for you, Sheryl. If you decide to leave and pursue other options, I'll take care of things here like selling the house. Guess we need to think about the cabin at the lake, too."

"Thanks, J.D. You're such a good brother. Now you must be getting back to your family."

"Yes, I know Stella wanted to be here, but it gets too complicated getting off the island quickly, especially with a couple of little ones. Stella's never been a great fan of the Goose." He was making reference to the amphibious float plane that took folks from Masset on the Charlottes to the mainland. Rather than having pontoons, the plane's front was shaped like the hull of a boat so it could take off from and land in the water, which splashed up over the windows.

"I don't blame her," said Sheryl. "I remember my trip out there that one summer after graduation. Give her, Abbey, and Lucy hugs for me. Maybe I'll get out there again someday."

"Well, I think I'm in position for a transfer soon. I'm not exactly sure where, but it may even be international. You take care of yourself, and call if you need anything." After one last hug, they parted with J.D. driving to Winnipeg for his first flight west.

Toward the end of the school year, Sheryl had come to the conclusion that she did need to make a change. Sitting on the deck of her family's cabin on Jackfish Lake as they had many times before, she and Penny had a glass of wine while discussing Sheryl's future.

"I've decided, Penny, that I'll go back to the University of North Dakota in Grand Forks to work on my master's."

She'd been in touch with the English Department, and as well as accepting her into their master's program, they had also offered her a position as a graduate teaching assistant to teach freshman composition classes.

"That will be a piece of cake," Sheryl continued. "At least it's no harder than teaching composition to our grade twelve students. Remember, when we graduated from high school, we were expected to already know how to write. You didn't have to take comp at Brandon U, but I did at UND because it was required.

The students down there hadn't written as much in high school as we did back in the day."

Penny sighed. "I'll miss you, Sheryl, but I understand, and I wish you all my best."

"We'll keep in touch," said Sheryl, giving her friend a hug.

"Of course," said Penny, but then she remembered how she and Ginny had said the same thing at the end of university, but they'd lost track of one another.

Once again, the best friends parted, and though Penny did make a couple of trips to Grand Forks that first year to see Sheryl, they eventually did lose track of one another. She couldn't even get in touch with J.D. to find out where Sheryl was. He had sold the drugstore, the house, and the cabin, and he was being posted in a variety of places across Canada and other countries. Nora and Ed had also left town, so she couldn't contact her through them either. Billy, like J.D., was all over the place. She'd lost track of him a long time ago, and because of her secret, she never even tried to find him.

CHAPTER
SEVENTEEN

Toward the end of the school year, just before Sheryl had left, a young family had moved to town. The man was the new bank manager. The Harrises had left years before after they'd lost their daughter, Grace, in childbirth, selling their house to Ed and Nora Stevens, who now also had left town. Early in the sixties, the Canadian Bank of Commerce and the Imperial Bank of Canada had merged to become the Canadian Imperial Bank of Commerce. CIBC had opened a new branch in Crocus Plains and sent Neil Campbell, one of their promising young managers, to get it started. He also brought his wife, Emily, and his two children, Corbin, a five-year-old, and Elizabeth, a toddler who was almost two years old.

When Penny went into the bank at the beginning of the summer to make sure her accounts were in order, the whole family happened to be in Neil's office, and she met them. Corbin was an athletic-looking little guy with blond hair and blue eyes. He came up to her and asked her where the swimming pool was.

"Uh, well, Corbin, we don't have a swimming pool, and we don't need one. Instead, we've got a terrific lake called Jackfish Lake, and it has a wonderful beach with a pier and lifeguards for swimming. Every year, the Red Cross also sponsors swimming lessons."

"Cool," Corbin responded. Turning to his mother, Emily, he asked, "Hey, Mom, can I take swimming lessons this year?"

"We'll see. We've got a lot going on this summer with our move, finding a house, and getting settled in," Emily responded.

"Maybe this lady Penny could take me," he said.

"Yeah, me too!" said his cute little sister, who had short, curly red hair. She ran to hug Penny.

"Aren't you a cutie, Elizabeth!" said Penny, picking up the little toddler and giving her a hug.

Putting her little arms around Penny's neck and giving her a squeeze, she said, "I'd like you to call me Libby."

"Boy, the kids have sure taken to you," said Neil. "Did you say you were a teacher?"

"Yes, I teach high school math. But I've always liked the little ones, and they do seem to like me."

"Are you working all summer?" asked Emily. "I could sure use some help with the kids while I get us organized. Have you ever worked as a summer nanny?"

"No, I haven't," said Penny, "but I have done occasional babysitting, and I am available this summer. I would certainly be happy to help you out."

"Yippee!" yelled Corbin, jumping up and down with Libby, holding her hand.

"Sounds like we've got a deal," said Emily. "We're staying in a hotel until we can find a house, so getting the kids out for other activities would be great."

"You've been such a help already, Penny," said Neil. "You don't by any chance know of any houses for sale, do you?"

"Actually, I do. My family was friends with another family all of our lives, and their daughter was my best friend growing up. Her parents have both passed away, and she has moved to the States. Her brother is in charge of selling their house. It's down Central Avenue near the elementary school, which would be perfect for you. They also have a lovely cabin out on the lake where we spent a lot of time together. If you like, I can give your contact information to the son so he can get in touch with you if you're interested. I might even be able to show you the places, as I think he left keys with my mum and dad in case there were interested folks and he couldn't get back here. He's in the military; I think he's posted in Ottawa now."

"That would be great, Penny. I can't believe how lucky we were that you stopped in today. If you ever need a loan or anything, just ask."

And thus began a long and close relationship between Penny and the Campbells. That summer she took the kids to the beach to swim. She sometimes brought them to her own little house to do crafts and play games. She also introduced them to the new children's television program *Mr. Dressup*. The main character donned a new costume each show and interacted with two puppets, Finnegan and Casey. Sitting in Penny's childhood rocking chair when the show would come on, Libby would point at the screen and shout out, "Oh, look! Case!" The kids also liked to go across the street to Penny's folks' place. Having no grandkids of their own, Will and Maudie loved having them around.

One day before swimming, Penny had them at the park near the beach, playing on the swings and seesaw. While there, Patty Warren came along with her little guy, Ben. Seeing Penny, Ben immediately ran to her for a hug. He was one of the little fellows she babysat.

"Hi, Patty and Ben. These are my friends Corbin and Libby." While Ben climbed on the end of the seesaw with Libby to balance it against Corbin, who was bigger and older than them both, Penny explained to Patty that they were the new banker's kids and that he was going to buy the Leighs' house and lake cabin.

"That's great. Looks like Ben and the kids have hit it off. Maybe we could have some playdates together," suggested Patty.

"Perfect, only better," agreed Penny.

A new relationship was begun among the three kids, but especially between Libby and Ben, who went through school together and eventually became sweethearts in high school.

In the meantime, Penny looked after the Campbell kids each summer and often helped out on weekends in the winter, too. At Christmastime, she would take them along with Ben to the Rainbow Theatre to the kids' show sponsored by the Elks Lodge, and they would visit Santa Claus afterward. Will was a member of the Elks, and for years Penny and Maudie had prepared all the little sacks of treats that Santa handed out to the kids after the movie.

Corbin became involved in the Mites hockey, so Penny would often take him to his Saturday morning practices, and then she would take both him and Libby to public skating in the afternoon.

Meanwhile, Principal Bradley was pushing her to get some administration classes under her belt. "Penny," he said, "I will retire one of these days, and you are the logical choice to replace me. I know it's not as easy for women to get principalships, so I want you to be well prepared. You are the best, and you deserve the position."

So she was trying to work in some administration classes at Brandon University during the summer. She also occasionally took night classes, which meant an hour's drive at night while still teaching and being the Campbell's part-time nanny, too.

By the time Corbin began high school, Penny had completed her administrative coursework and was ready to take on the principal's position when Mr. Bradley retired in a few years. Penny had become Corbin's role model even though she was a woman. Rather than being a banker like his father, Corbin wanted to become a math teacher and then maybe a principal, too. He'd become quite the hockey player as well, so he thought he might even be able to coach while teaching as well. During the summer, he also had started lifeguarding at the Jackfish Lake beach.

Corbin was in grade twelve when Libby and Ben entered grade nine. Watching the three of them at the Freshie dance brought back a lot of memories of herself, Sheryl, Diane, Marsy, Bernie, and Roger. Then, of course, there was Billy who, like Corbin, was in grade twelve. Although it was unknown to her at the time, Billy was her big brother, like Corbin was to Libby. When Ben and Libby waltzed cheek to cheek for the last dance, her old feelings for Billy surfaced. They were impossible to deny even though they had been impossible to follow in life.

Soon Corbin was off to university, and he started spending summers at Clear Lake as a lifeguard. Clear Lake, in northern Manitoba, was a popular spot for high school and college-aged students to make money during the summer. Libby and Ben would soon follow him once they graduated high school and went off to Brandon University.

Penny had just become the principal of Crocus Plains Collegiate Institute when Corbin finished his math degree and teacher certification program. He wanted to teach for his mentor and hero, Penny Ryan. Fortunately, a position had opened in the math department, and she made sure he at least got an interview. The other math instructors remembered him as a student and were impressed with his success at Brandon U, so he became a part of Penny's first faculty as principal.

By then, Ben and Libby were at Brandon University. Libby wanted to be an English teacher, and Ben wanted to get his degree in science and then become a pharmacist. He hoped someday he'd be able to take over Leigh's Drugstore and Libby could teach English at the high school. They would settle back in Crocus Plains, get married, and raise a family with grandparents nearby.

CHAPTER EIGHTEEN

*L*eigh's Drugstore had finally been purchased by a new pharmacist. Being new to Crocus Plains, Rodney Hughes kept the original name so that customers who had known the Leighs would be drawn to his store. A new pharmacy had come to town across the street a few years back and had become well established, but Crocus Plains served a farming community within a large area of farms and small villages, so he felt there was room for them both.

Penny happened to go into the drugstore one day to check things out and pick up some vitamins, bandages, gauze, peroxide, and a few other things to replenish her first aid kit at the house. She introduced herself to Rodney.

"Hi, I'm Penny Ryan, the principal at the collegiate. More importantly, I was best friends with the daughter of the Leighs. They were a great family. Welcome to Crocus Plains."

Holding out his hand to shake hers, he said, "Pleased to meet you, Penny. My name is Rodney Hughes, and I hope I can provide the community with service as well as the Leighs did."

"I'm sure you will. The folks here have been waiting a long time for someone to reopen the store. Well, nice meeting you, and good luck."

As Penny turned to leave, Rodney, who was attracted to her friendly face, warm brown eyes, and reddish-highlighted brown hair, said, "Uh, since I'm new here, I don't know much about the area. I could use someone to help me learn about it. Would you consider going for dinner some evening and let me ply you with questions?"

"Sure, I could do that. I imagine you'll be open Saturday night. That's when all the area farm families come to town, so how about Sunday evening? I could meet you at Bakker's Beach Barbecue at seven o'clock on Sunday."

"I could pick you up if you tell me where you live."

"Oh, that won't be necessary. I may be working at the school earlier, so it's probably easier to just plan to meet you." Even though he was a businessman in town, she didn't know him that well, and she thought it safer to provide her own transportation.

Penny was able to spend Sunday at home, unlike what she had told Rodney, but she was still glad she would be meeting him rather than having him pick her up and bring her home. One never knew what such an arrangement could lead to. Bakker's Barbecue was a casual restaurant where she had worked in her youth, so she knew she didn't have to get too fancy in her dress. It was a cool fall night, so she donned khaki slacks and a blue denim shirt topped with a brown suede blazer. She accented her outfit with a blue, brown, and tan floral scarf twisted around her neck a couple of times then tied in a knot, the ends spreading out almost like petals. She twisted her hair up into a roll, holding it with a gold comb that allowed curls to flow over it. Putting on gold earrings and smoothing coral lipstick over her mouth, she looked at her appearance reflected in the mirror.

She nodded her head approvingly, thinking, *Not too formal, not too sexy. Casual. Shouldn't give any wrong impressions.* She grabbed her purse and her keys and headed out the door to her car. She was surprised to see Will, her father, out by the car, cleaning the windows.

"Hi, Dad. What are you doing?"

"I've noticed the bugs are really hitting the windows these days, especially in the evening. I just cleaned our Galaxie 500, so thought I might as well do yours, too." Stepping back and taking a good look at her, he continued, "Oh, it looks like you're going somewhere. Looking pretty cool, as your students would say. Where are you going?"

She explained the plan for the evening. Looking at her with affection but still with the concern of a father, he said, "Well, have a good evening. Don't stay out too late. Tomorrow is a school day. Good thing I cleaned your windows. They would be worse by the time you get home, especially in the evening down by the lake."

"Yes, Daddy," she laughed. "I'll be a good girl. Thanks for cleaning the windows. Give Mum a hug for me."

He started across the street, looking back at his daughter and waving at her as she climbed into the car. Back in the house, Will told Maudie about their daughter's sort-of date. "I wonder why she's never found the love of her life like I found you, Maudie. I still don't know why she pushed Billy out of her life. They seemed like a perfect match."

"I agree, Will, but Nora sure never thought so. I don't know why she didn't like Penny for her son. Probably because Penny's my daughter and Nora never did completely warm up to me. Anyway, that's all in the past. Maybe tonight will be the turning point for Penny."

Walking into the restaurant and seeing Rodney hop up immediately to pull out her chair for her, Penny began thinking the same thing her mother had.

"Good evening, Penny. You look gorgeous. So perfect for a fall prairie night."

Penny pulled her head back, looking at him with her eyebrows pulled together in a question. Certainly "gorgeous" hadn't been her aim. Was he just a smooth talker?

Seeing Penny's suspicious look, Rodney hurriedly said, "Sorry, I didn't mean to upset you, but you really are an attractive woman, and you know just how to accent it, even for a casual date like tonight."

Her eyebrows suddenly rose in surprise. Rodney started to laugh. "I guess we'd better look at the menu instead of listening to my goofy attempts at being complimentary."

Feeling more comfortable now that he was being humorous, Penny grinned and started going over the menu, recommending her favourites to help him make his choice. From then on, the evening went smoothly. Penny answered all his questions as best she could to help him understand the area and the people in it. He'd come from Winnipeg, so small-town living was unfamiliar to him.

After their grilled chicken, mashed sweet potatoes, and corn on the cob arrived, Penny observed Rodney a little more closely as she savored her dinner. She really hadn't noticed before that he was handsome. His thick black hair was well groomed and smoothed back Elvis Presley style. His sculptured cheekbones and Roman nose enhanced his full lips. Penny wondered if they made him a good kisser. He was dressed much like her: casual, yet very neat and attractive. He looked intelligent and like a leader. *Hmmm*, she thought. *He could be a community leader at some point.*

After they'd finished their meal and were enjoying their coffee, the waitress came to tell them they were closing up for the night. They quickly gulped down some coffee, Rodney paid the bill, and they walked out the door. He walked Penny to her car and waited while she unlocked it. "Thank you for the nice evening," he said. "I hope it won't be the last one."

"Thank you for dinner, and I'm sure we'll get together again." She hopped in her Datsun before the moment got uncomfortable and drove home.

* * *

As the school year progressed, Penny recognized more each day how valuable Corbin was to the students, the faculty, and her. Like she had been to Principal Bradley, Corbin was becoming her right-hand man, a great assistant. She could see that someday she'd be encouraging him to start taking administration classes. This was his first year teaching, and she wanted him to have the time to feel comfortable and at his best there. He seemed like a natural, however, so that wouldn't take long. She also noticed that a lot of the young women teachers were hanging around him a lot.

Penny smiled to herself, recalling how he had always brought home a different girl for weekends in Crocus Plains while he was going to Brandon University. Libby had told her that it got so frequent that it had become the family joke when he'd show up with a new one to say, "Do we have to learn this one's name?" knowing that they'd probably never see her again. Corbin was an attractive guy but a respectful one, too. He never took advantage of all the young woman chasing him.

Thinking about attractive guys, Penny often had Rodney come to mind. They had been seeing one another frequently on a casual basis, meeting for coffee, a drink at the pub that was now open to women, too, or a ride around town during which Penny would point out where folks lived. On one of these last rides, Penny brought him to her little house. She explained how it had been the home her father had brought his English war bride to, and that she had been raised in it until her grandparents had passed away and they'd moved across the street into their house.

Penny pulled a bottle of red wine from the fridge and got Rod, as she now called him, to open it while she cut some cheese slices to have with crackers. Bringing the items into the small living room, Penny placed the snacks on the little coffee table and started to sit in the chair next to the couch, where Rod was sitting.

"Penny." Rod's voice stopped her motion. "Please come and join me here," he said, patting the cushioned place beside him. "We can both reach the snacks better then."

Penny grinned at him, acknowledging that she didn't believe that was the real reason he was patting the couch. She did, however, move over to the couch, sliding in behind the table and sitting beside him.

They talked a bit while they nibbled on the cheese and crackers and sipped their wine. Penny wondered where this might all lead. They had had a few casual goodnight kisses but nothing deeply passionate.

As if he were reading her mind, Rod slid one arm around the back of her shoulders while his other went around her waist, pulling her closer to him. "Penny," he said, looking deeply into her eyes, "I think I'm falling for you." Then he leaned in and kissed her deeply, running his tongue around her lips until she opened her mouth, welcoming him in for an even deeper, more passionate kiss.

That evening was the beginning of an affectionate and more intimate relationship as the year went on. By Christmas, they had started discussing how intimate they should get and how they should handle it.

Over the holidays, Libby and Ben were home from university. Watching them at the New Year's Eve dance at the Legion, Penny could tell their love was growing even deeper. She wondered how they were handling intimacy when they still had university to finish. She was surprised when she had the chance to visit with Libby alone for a few minutes one day before they left to go back to university. Libby confided in her that she and Ben were soul mates and that they were expressing their love physically. She had seen a doctor in Brandon and gotten on the pill so they wouldn't start a family too soon.

Penny wondered if she should do that, too. Maybe she and Rod could talk about it the next night when they were together for New Year's Day.

The subject actually came up earlier than the next evening. When Rod arrived at her place for dinner at noon, he immediately pulled her into his arms and kissed her repeatedly and passionately. Pulling away at one point, Penny said, "Rod, I think we need to talk."

"Don't you like my loving you?" he asked.

"Of course I do. Too much so, and that's why we have to discuss how we're going to handle it since we are both professionals and don't want to ruin things with an accident. I was thinking I should go on the pill."

"No, you can't do that. I'm Catholic, and that's against my religion."

"What about condoms?"

"Same thing. But I don't really want to have children. Not just now—not ever."

"Really?" Penny asked in shock.

"I know you like kids and you're good with them, but I think they'd just take away from our life together and the freedom to travel and use our money on things other than their activities and education."

"I didn't realize you thought that way. How are we going to prevent a pregnancy then? Abstinence? A platonic relationship?" Penny asked, doubt about their relationship rising in her mind. She still hoped that if they married, he'd change his mind.

"Catholics use withdrawal effectively. You understand that process, don't you?"

"Well, yes, I do, but that puts a lot of pressure and responsibility on you to get out in time."

"I know, but it'd be worth it. Wanna try it now?" he asked, grinning seductively.

"No. I think I need a bit of time to process the idea."

They left it at that for the time being, but a few weeks later, things got a little out of control in their lovemaking. The fore-play had been so stimulating, Penny was anxious to pull him into her, but she left it up to him. Rod had the same feelings, and he entered her. While she was going over the top with an orgasm, he withdrew before he let things go.

"See, it works," he said to her.

"For now, anyway," she added, a note of doubt in her tone.

Their relationship continued, growing deeper in commit-ment even if their intimacy was unstable.

Soon it was summer and school was out for everyone. Corbin had continued to lifeguard at Clear Lake during the summers, while he taught during the school year. Now that Libby and Ben were in university, they'd decided to join Corbin at Clear Lake. Ben got a job at a boat rental place, and Libby was going to wait tables at one of the main street restaurants. Together they found a cabin they could all rent. Suspicious, but not completely in the know, Emily and Neil Campbell were glad the three were together, hoping that having her big brother there would prevent Libby and Ben from going all the way. The Campbells were too late to prevent anything, but Ben and Libby were truly in love, and they were mature and responsible about their relationship.

Rod, of course, still had to work all summer at his store, but Penny had the summer off, though she continued to research and make plans for continually improving the collegiate for Crocus Plains. She had much more free time than during the school year, so when Rod was ready for time together, so was she. Their relationship had grown deeper. On July 1 after the Canada Day celebration, while they were watching the nighttime fireworks over the lake, Rod pulled a little box from his pocket, opened it, and handed it to Penny. At that moment, the explosion of light from the last fireworks send-off emphasized the sparkle in the diamond. Penny looked at it with amazement. Then Rod asked her, "Penny, will you marry me? I want us to be together forever."

Stunned, she whispered, "Yes, of course." Rod then took the ring from its box and placed it on her ring finger. Later, they made plans to marry during the Christmas holiday season, and they celebrated their future union with their typical physical union that night.

Everyone was excited about their news when they shared it the next day, especially Will and Maudie, who had hoped Penny would find a true love so they could become grandparents. Corbin, Libby, and Ben were also excited for them when they heard the news after they returned home from their summer jobs. "It will be our turn next," said Ben, squeezing Libby closer to him.

The summer passed, and soon Libby and Ben were back at Brandon University. Corbin and Penny had the collegiate well prepared for the first day of school after the Labour Day weekend.

The fall days were beautiful, with warm days, cool nights, and the beauty of the multicoloured leaves. Canadian Thanksgiving was in October, and it was exceptionally warm for the season; snow had not fallen yet. Rodney convinced Penny to escape for the long weekend to a friend's cabin on Pelican Lake. It was a gorgeous setting, and the wine Rod had brought to drink by the fireplace made it especially romantic. Their wedding date was swiftly approaching, and their affection for one another was growing deeper each day. When they fell into bed the second night of the weekend, the passion of their intimacy was so deep that there was no holding back. Not being able to control himself, Rod went the whole way, and Penny reacted to his explosion with an explosion of her own, having an orgasm like she'd never experienced before.

"That was wonderful," she said, looking into her future husband's eyes.

"Unbelievable," he agreed, then added, "but remember, we have to be careful. We can't do it all the time."

"But what difference would an accident make? We're getting married."

"I know. But you know my personal feelings about kids, Penny."

She'd hoped he'd change his mind. Disappointed, she rolled over and tried to go to sleep. So much was going through her brain, but she pretended to be sleeping because she couldn't face him right now.

A couple of weeks later, her period was due, but it didn't come. She figured it was just going to be a day or two late, but she'd also been feeling a little queasy. She'd put that down to a touch of stomach flu that was going around. Penny got out her calendar, figured out the date they'd truly gone all the way, and counted it against the date of her expected period. She was as regular as clockwork, so that was easy. Then the results hit her. Their special night had been right in the middle of the fertile days of her cycle. She was pregnant.

How was she going to tell Rod? How would he take it? Surely now that there was a real little person on its way, he'd change his mind. Maybe he'd even be a bit excited. Then she remembered she was the principal of the collegiate and that this would not be good for her career; in fact, she might lose her job. She wouldn't want to be a bad role model for the students. They could move their wedding date up. It was early in the pregnancy, so if they eloped over the coming weekend, it might be acceptable, especially since everyone knew they were engaged. Even if she lost her job, so be it. Being a mother to this little creation from their love would be more important than a job. They could live on Rod's income until things worked out. Anyway, the next step was to tell Rodney.

It was Saturday, so she knew Rodney would be at the drugstore all day. Now that winter was around the corner, the stores no longer stayed open on Saturday evenings, so she could see him that night. How was she going to tell him? What would his reaction be? These thoughts swirled around in her head all day. At one point, she called him at the store to let him know she'd come to his place after supper. He was delighted.

At seven o'clock, she donned her Cowichan sweater and drove to his apartment. "Hello, baby!" he said as he opened the door to his suite and pulled her into his arms for a big hug. "So glad you decided to come tonight. I've got a plan for us." He grinned down at her. Penny hoped his happy attitude would carry them through the revelation of her purpose for being there.

She pulled away slightly and, smiling up at him, responded, "Well, I've got some plans, too, for discussion. I've got some big news that might lead into other plans. Can we sit down and talk for a bit?"

"Sure. Come on over to my love seat." As they sat down on the cozy seat, he added, "Perfect. Just room for the two of us."

"Actually, there's room for three of us. That's what I've come to talk to you about. Rod, I'm pregnant."

Shocked, he said, "What? How could that happen?"

Trying to keep the tone light, she giggled a little and responded, "Come on, Rod, you're a pharmacist with a biology background. You know how it happens."

"Don't be silly. We've avoided this happening. At least, I've done my part."

"I'm afraid not one hundred percent. Remember the weekend at Pelican Lake?"

His shoulders sank as he recalled it. It had been a wonderful lovemaking evening, but now they were paying the price. Well, there were solutions.

"We can't have this baby. First of all, this news would ruin your career, and second, you know I have no desire to have kids. I just want you."

"But we're engaged. If we get married in the next few days, like tomorrow, there wouldn't be a problem with my job. And our baby would be born with married parents and given our family name."

"You still don't get it, Penny. I don't want this baby. We'll have to get rid of it."

"What do you mean? I'd have to give it up for adoption?"

"No. Abortion is now legal in Canada, and I have contacts I can use. We can go away to have it done as soon as possible. No one will ever have to know you were pregnant."

"But you're Catholic! That's against your religion, just like birth control."

"But you're not! And aren't you women always fighting for your free choice?"

"Your proposal is not my choice. I want this baby. It was made with love, and I want it to live with love."

"Sorry, Penny, but here's your choice. It's me or the baby."

"I can't believe you said that. Aren't you the man I thought you were?"

"I am. I told you no kids. So there's your choice."

Getting up from the love seat, Penny walked to the door, saying, "I can't deal with this right now."

Jumping up from his position, Rodney yelled, "Wait! We have to make a plan now before it's too late." Before he got to the door, Penny walked through it, slamming it behind her.

Tears flowed down her cheeks as she drove home. What man wouldn't take responsibility for his actions? Yet he expected her to go against her own beliefs and desires. Did she really know him? No, she decided, she didn't. He was a man who had to be in control.

She avoided seeing him for a couple of days, but during that time, she'd had some strange feelings in her stomach and abdomen area. It wasn't the morning sickness feeling like she'd had at first. She was feeling a lot of stress. Maybe it was that. He had given her a choice, but there really wasn't one. She wanted this baby, and she didn't think she wanted Rod anymore. But that meant she'd have to make a lot more decisions for herself as a single parent.

On the evening of the second day after they'd had their confrontation, she started feeling excruciating pain in her abdomen. What was happening? She didn't want to be alone, but she couldn't call her parents and put them through all this. She called Marylynn, a new friend she'd made who'd recently moved to Crocus Plains to work in the hospital. She was a nurse.

Marylynn immediately came flying over to Penny's house. Penny had left the door unlocked so she could come right in. It was a good thing, because when Marylynn opened the door, Penny was in the bathroom sitting on the toilet, bent over and holding her stomach in excruciating pain.

Seeing Marylynn, Penny said, "I think I'm having a vicious bowel movement. Stuff is plopping in the toilet."

Coming over to Penny, Marylynn put her hand on Penny's back and looked behind her into the bowl. "Penny, it's blood flowing out of you! Have you been having intestinal issues?"

Sinking even lower over her knees, Penny explained to her friend that she was a few weeks pregnant.

"Oh, Penny. I'm so sorry. I think you've just miscarried. I think we'd better go to the emergency room for you to get checked out."

"I can't," Penny said. "No one knows about this, and I don't want to ruin my life more than I already have."

"There are privacy ethics in the medical field, Penny. The doctor who sees you will tell no one. I think Dr. Stanley is on tonight, and he will be perfect. You have lost a little life, but we have to make sure you survive. I'll be with you the whole way."

Indeed, Dr. Stanley was wonderful. As well as knowing his stuff and confirming Penny's miscarriage, he was patient, under-standing, and sympathetic. He gave her treatment and allowed her to go home as long as Marylynn would stay with her all night. Marylynn took Penny in a wheelchair to her car, drove her home, and tucked her into bed, giving her the sleeping pill Dr. Stanley had provided. She then curled up on Penny's couch and pulled the afghan over herself, knowing she probably wouldn't be able to sleep at all.

The next morning, Penny felt better physically but was emo-tionally drained, so she called in sick to the school. She knew Corbin could take care of things. Marylynn stayed with her through the morning to make sure Penny was all right, then left at noon to sleep and prepare for her evening shift. Penny couldn't thank her enough for being there for her.

Alone, Penny cried every time she thought about her loss. Regardless of Rod's feelings, she had wanted to be that baby's mother, and she would have raised it alone if that's the way it had to be. Would this miscarriage keep her from ever getting preg-nant again? Of course, she would never be able to have a baby as long as she was with Rod. Now what was she going to do about him? He wasn't the man she'd thought he was.

That evening, a knock came to her door. Forgetting she was on the evening shift, Penny thought it was Marylynn checking on her again. Penny opened the door to find Rodney standing there.

"I heard you were sick and not at school today. Thought I should check on you. Can I come in?"

"For a minute," Penny replied, barely letting him inside the door. After shutting it, she didn't invite him in further. She explained, "I had a miscarriage. I lost our baby last night." A tear trickled down her cheek.

"That's great, Penny!" Rodney exclaimed. "Don't cry. Our problems are all solved. You don't have to have an abortion, and we won't have a baby. It was perfect timing. Now we can go ahead with our original plans to marry in December and have a wonderful life together, just the two of us."

Penny couldn't believe what she was hearing. His reaction only confirmed he wasn't the man she thought he was. "No, Rod. We won't be getting married. I don't know you anymore, so I definitely don't want to live my whole life with you." Pulling off her ring, she put it in the pocket of his shirt, not wanting to touch his hand. "We are done. Please leave now."

"Wait, Penny. You can't mean this. Let's talk."

"Oh, I definitely mean this. You are not going to control my life. Now get out of here before I call the Mounties." She opened the door and slightly pushed him so he'd know she meant business.

* * *

Everyone was shocked that the couple had broken up. Will and Maudie couldn't understand what could possibly have happened, and they began to wonder about their daughter's ability to maintain a relationship. Penny hadn't gone into any details about the situation, but their continuous questioning and concern made her feel that at some point she might have to tell them her story.

Rod's male pride wouldn't allow him to say Penny had been the one to break it off, so she also remained vague when questioned in order to protect his pride and reputation. It was a little more difficult when she had to face Libby over the Christmas holidays.

"I don't get it, Penny," Libby exclaimed. "I came home expecting to attend your wedding. You have always been my role model, and your love for and marriage to Rodney were what Ben and I were aiming for after we graduate."

"I'm sorry to let you down, Libby, but sometimes things just aren't meant to be." Little did Libby know that someday she would be saying the same thing.

CHAPTER
NINETEEN

Penny got through the rest of the school year with Corbin being her right-hand man. Sensing something wasn't quite right with Penny, he took on even more responsibility. Finally, Penny took him aside one day and said, "Corbin, you've been such a wonderful assistant to me, almost like a vice principal. You really need to start taking some administration courses at the university during the summers instead of lifeguarding. I know you enjoy being at Clear Lake, and I'm sure the extra income is helpful, but I think I can get the school board to give you some assistance with your course fees when they realize the school's benefit in the future."

"What about Libby and Ben? I think the folks expect me to be their overseer and supervisor."

Smiling at him and remembering what Libby had told her about birth control, she replied, "I think Libby and Ben are more than capable of looking after themselves, Corbin. They may even like having some solitude."

Corbin laughed, well aware of his sister and Ben's love. "Okay, you're right. I'll look into the courses that are being offered this summer. I could maybe take some evening courses during the school year, but I'm kind of committed to coaching the Midget hockey team, and I still like to play with the senior men's league, too."

"Great. I'll approach the school board at their next meeting."

And so began Corbin's preparation for being a principal someday and Ben and Libby's precious summers alone in preparation for their lifetime love together. Occasionally, Corbin would go up to Clear Lake on a weekend to see them and substitute for the lifeguards if they needed extra help.

The summer after their graduation—before Libby's certification preparation year and Ben's beginning into pharmacy—their lives and love were changed forever.

One of the neighbours renting a cabin near Ben and Libby complained to Ben about the way his boat was operating. "The motor isn't sounding right. Since you're working with boats every day at the rental place, I thought maybe you might have an idea of what's going on."

"Today's my day off, so I could take it for a run and see if I can figure out what the problem is," Ben suggested. The neighbour was appreciative and handed him the keys to the boat.

Even though Ben was very adept at handling boats, he forgot to turn the blower on to remove any gas fumes that were in the engine compartment before starting up the motor. Turning the key created sparks in the engine compartment, and a sudden explosion blew up the boat, tossing Ben into the air, then deep into the water. Due to injuries from the explosion, he was unable to bring himself to the surface, and he drowned before he could be saved.

Corbin happened to be there that weekend, and standing on the wharf, he saw the accident. He jumped into the rescue boat going to the accident site and was the one to dive into the lake and bring Ben's body to the surface. Holding Ben in his arms as the rescue boat and first responders took them back to shore, Corbin cried silently to himself, realizing that telling his sister was going to be an even harder rescue.

Corbin pulled himself together and made the arrangements for Ben's body to be taken home to Crocus Plains. He then called his parents, Neil and Emily, asking them to break the news to Ben's mother, Patty Warren. Finally, he went to the restaurant where Libby was waiting tables. He explained to the owner what had happened, saying that he had to take his sister home and that she probably wouldn't be back that summer.

"Come on, Libby, we need to go home for the weekend," Corbin said to his sister.

"I can't, Corbin," Libby responded. "I'm busy here, and Ben and I have plans for tonight."

The restaurant owner interrupted, saying that it was fine and they'd manage. Eyebrows pulled together as she wondered what was going on, Libby left with her brother, but the minute they got in his car, she plied him with questions. He asked her to wait until they got to the cabin where she was staying.

After he told her about the accident, Libby fell apart. "I can't believe this. I can't stay here. I can't live without him."

Corbin tried comforting her, saying, "Ben wouldn't want to hear you say that. But you won't have to stay here. Pack a few things you'll need so we can head home right away. I'll come back with you another day to pack up your things, and Ben's for his mother. In fact, I'll come by myself if you just can't do it."

A few days after the funeral, Libby went to visit Penny. She fell into her arms and sobbed. Penny had been her nanny, her education mentor, and her surrogate big sister. Penny let Libby share all her emotions, and in the end she encouraged her to complete her certification year. "Ben would want you to do it, Libby," Penny said, drawing on the only possible argument that Libby might follow, because it was the truth.

It was a difficult year, and Libby struggled through it. The only thing that kept her going was her weekend visits with her parents, her brother Corbin, and Penny, who promised there would be a job waiting for when she finished her program.

Everyone thought her coming back to Crocus Plains to teach would be the best way for her to recover after losing Ben. As it turned out, working with teenagers in the school where she and Ben had fallen in love as adolescents flooded her with too many memories that almost destroyed her. She felt she couldn't stay.

Becky, one of her classmates in the teacher certification program, was from Victoria, British Columbia, and had gone back there to teach. They had kept in touch, and when Becky found out Libby needed a change, she called her to tell her about a job opening for an English teacher in Masset, British Columbia, up on the Queen Charlotte Islands off the northwest coast of Canada.

Libby talked to Penny about it. "It's apparently very remote, almost isolated, but maybe that's what I need: a completely unique experience. Mum and Dad and I have kind of skirted the issue of actually talking about Ben. I think they believe that avoiding the subject will help me forget, but being back here and reliving the past has just increased my pain. I'm not going to tell them that's the reason I'm leaving because I know they'll just worry more. I'll tell them I'm looking on it as a new adventure."

"I understand your logic and appreciate your trying to protect them, but I think it's hard for parents not to worry anyway. I know mine still worry about me no matter how I try to assure them. Anyway, Libby, you have to do what's right for you. I understand how difficult it must be to be here without Ben," said Penny, thinking to herself how difficult it was to see Rod almost every day in town but being without him because being together would never work.

"Thanks for understanding, Penny. You've always been there for me ever since I was a toddler. I'll really miss you, but I'll keep in touch."

* * *

Libby did write a few times the first few months she was on the Charlottes. She seemed to be settling into the new culture of the military presence, the local logging and commercial fishing families, and especially the proud and talented Haida First Nation. She'd made friends with a French-Canadian teacher who was married to a military medical officer. She also frequently mentioned Dr. Shirlee, who ran a coffee shop and used book store called Dr. Shirlee's Books 'n' Brew. In one letter, Libby wrote, *She reminds me a lot of you, Penny. She's been a mentor and is really supportive. I think I could talk to her about anything, just like you.*

Libby's parents continued to worry about her, as did Patty Warren, Ben's mother. Near the Christmas holiday season, Patty told Penny she was going to write to Libby, hoping to relieve some of Libby's pain by letting her know Ben would want both Libby and his mum to carry on in life.

Trying to get her own life back to normal, Penny sat in a local restaurant bar, having a glass of wine with Marylynn and the new hairdresser, Gloria, who'd opened a salon in town. They were toasting one another and the holiday season when two men came in and joined them. They were Penny's lifetime friends, Bernie and Roger. She introduced them to her new friends.

School had closed for the holidays, and soon another younger couple came into the lounge. It was Corbin with a flashy blond hanging on his arm. Penny recognized her as one of the tellers at his father's bank. Remembering Libby's joking about her brother, Penny grinned at Corbin and told the couple to join them at their table.

"Is Libby coming home for Christmas?" Penny asked as soon as they sat down.

"No. I don't think she's quite ready to come back," Corbin replied, looking a bit wistful. Penny realized that Corbin probably understood the real reason she'd escaped to the islands.

Penny spent a quiet Christmas with her parents. They reminisced about the years they used to celebrate with the Leigh and Stevens families. "I still don't get why you split up with Billy," Will said, frowning at his daughter.

"Oh, some things just are never meant to be, Dad," Penny responded, using her standard line for all the separations from men she'd experienced in life. The conversation made her wonder whatever had happened to Billy and where Sheryl was now. "I guess we won't be going to the New Year's Eve dance at the Legion like we used to either," Penny laughed, remembering more past fun times.

"There's no reason why you can't go!" encouraged Maudie, wishing her daughter would open herself to life's possibilites.

The holidays were soon over, and Penny plunged herself back into the job she loved, which made up for anything else missing in her life. The school year passed quickly, and toward its end, Corbin approached her and said, "Libby's coming home as soon as school is over, and I don't think she's going back. I'm not sure what happened, but she's wondering if there would be a job for her here next fall."

"Really? That does seem strange. I'm sure we can find something for her to do even if it's subbing until something opens up," Penny assured him.

* * *

A few weeks later, Libby did arrive back in Crocus Plains, but not alone. A handsome young man accompanied her. His dark curly hair and bronze skin tone gave him an exotic look. In contrast, he also had startlingly blue eyes. It turned out that his father had been Caucasian and his mother was Haida. His name was Connor Ferguson, and he was both a provincial medical doctor and a skilled pilot. He and Libby were planning a small, quick wedding; then they'd return to the Queen Charlotte Islands to make their home.

These plans were very different from what Corbin had told Penny before school had ended, so she was hoping to have the opportunity to have a private personal chat with Libby. That opportunity arose when a knock on the door of Penny's small white house brought her face-to-face with Libby.

"Libby!" Penny exclaimed, drawing her into her arms. "How great to see you. It's been so long."

"Yes, it has, Penny. I've missed you so much, too. You've always been there for me, and there were certainly times when I needed you on the islands this past year. For that reason, I'd love it if you would be my personal attendant for our wedding."

"Of course, Libby. I'd be honoured. But tell me, what is happening? Corbin said you were coming home to stay and were hoping for a position at the collegiate. Now that all seems to have changed."

Libby then told Penny the story of how she'd met Connor the first day she'd arrived in Masset on the islands. As their paths kept crossing, an attraction had arisen between them. When she got Patty's letter at Christmas, it gave her the okay to be open again to love—and love they did.

"But that wasn't the end of challenges and issues within our relationship. I somehow got under the impression that Connor had a longtime love with a Haida woman, who turned out to be his half-sister. With that misunderstanding and his thinking he was going to always be in competition with my memory of Ben, I backed away from the relationship. That's when I remembered your saying once that sometimes things just aren't meant to be. Anyway, during this time I realized I was pregnant, but I couldn't

147

tell him because I didn't want him to feel obligated to marry me. That's when I decided to come home. But Connor discovered on his own that I was pregnant, and when he finally realized the baby was his, he met me at the airport, and said he was coming home with me because he loves me and our baby needs both a mother and a father. So that's my story, and I'm sticking to it."

Libby laughed for a moment with Penny. Then, looking at her mentor with sad eyes, she quickly continued, "Are you disappointed in me, Penny, for getting pregnant before marriage?"

Penny pulled Libby into her arms to comfort her as she had many times before. Remembering her own pregnancy, miscarriage, and Rod, she replied, "Of course not, Libby. I think this baby was created from love. Connor is a good man, and it seems that he will be a great husband and father."

"Thank you, Penny. You always were understanding. I'm sorry you've never found true love."

"As I've said before, and I'll say it again, I guess some things are just never meant to be."

Smiling at her, Libby said, "I'm so glad you're going to be able to meet our good friends Stephen and Aimée Parker. Stephen was with the military, and now that they are pulling out of the islands, he's going to stay and practice medicine at the new regional clinic and hospital with Connor. I taught with Aimée at the high school, and now we're both pregnant, so we'll raise our babies together. They will stand up with Connor and me at the ceremony. Connor's sister is also coming with them for the wedding. Actually, the three of them played an important role in Connor and I getting back together."

"Sounds like you've really made a good life and home for yourself on the Charlottes, Libby. I am so happy for you. I am also thrilled to be a part of the celebration. Now, what are some things I can do for you to get ready?"

"One of the main things I need is someone to do my hair. I'm wearing Mum's wedding dress, so that's all taken care of. Is there a beauty salon in town now?"

"Yes, there is. I know just the perfect person to work on your beautiful strawberry blond hair. She owns Gloria's Glamour, and she will indeed make you glamourous!"

And so the wedding plans began, and the following Saturday, the event took place at the United Church, with a small reception at the pavilion down by the lake. Penny enjoyed meeting the Parkers and was quite entertained by Aimée's sense of humour. Penny thought Willow, Connor's half-sister, was a beautiful, intelligent woman, and she would have loved to spend more time with her learning about the Haida culture. Looking over at Corbin, who had a pretty brunette hanging all over him, Penny wished he could find someone like Willow instead of the floozies who were forever chasing him.

It had been a beautiful wedding for a beautiful couple. Two days later, Libby and Connor left with their friends and sister to return to the Misty Isles, as the Charlottes were nicknamed, to begin their lifetime together in Masset.

CHAPTER
TWENTY

*B*ack at school in the fall, Penny and Corbin reminisced about the wedding and their happiness for Libby, who had found true love on the Misty Isles.

"Yeah, she's a lucky one," said Corbin. "Not like you and me, Penny. I don't know if we'll ever find what she has. We don't seem to be lucky in love."

"Well, Corbin, Libby would probably remind you that she hasn't always been lucky in love either." Remembering Ben, Corbin bent his head down in sadness and nodded it in agreement. Penny continued, saying, "I think there were some twists and turns in her and Connor's relationship development, too."

"I kind of got that impression, too," Corbin said. "She may have revealed more to you."

"Maybe, but right now we've got work to do to get ready for opening day. By the way, congratulations on finishing your administration course. You are now ready to be a principal. I appreciate having you as my VP, and someday I will recommend you for taking on my position when I retire."

"I appreciate that, Penny. I've learned a lot from you. Not just about teaching and administering in schools, but about life also. You've been a role model for me ever since I was five years old."

"Thanks, Corbin. Both you and Libby had lots of talent and character, so it was easy to be around you and lead you. How do your folks feel about Libby being so far away and missing out on being close to their first grandchild?"

"Oh, they'll be making many trips up to the islands to visit them. In fact, they're thinking about retirement in the next year or so. They've always wanted to have a place in Arizona for the winter, but then they will also be freer to go to the Charlottes to see Libby and her family. Who knows, now that the military is withdrawing from the islands, maybe they'll even buy a PMQ for a summer retreat. Oh, PMQ means 'private married quarters,' in other words, a house for military families. Stephen Parker explained that to me."

"That would be great. Then they'd have lots of time to spend with a grandchild or children, and maybe they could even babysit if they were there for the summer. I imagine you'll want to take a few trips up, too. I know I'd like to."

Within a few years, Neil and Emily Campbell did retire, and they found a winter retreat in Arizona. They also visited Libby, Connor, and baby Zach during the summer months. When baby number two was on the way, they made plans to spend time with the family to help out. They hadn't considered a permanent summer retreat in Masset, but there were a lot more places to rent than there had been when Libby had first arrived on the islands. They were, however, thinking about a cabin at Clear Lake for summers.

With his family all gone and no love of his own, Corbin was starting to look around for a principalship of his own. There was no serious romantic interest or family to hold him back in Crocus Plains and wait for Penny to retire. He liked helping her, but he thought having a school of his own would prepare him better for her position when it came open.

About six years after Libby and Connor were married, Libby contacted her brother to let him know that the high school in Masset was looking for a new principal, telling him they would love to have him close by to watch his nephew and the new baby grow up.

Corbin was very tempted by the opportunity, but he felt he should talk about it with Penny. Explaining the situation, he said, "I have mixed feelings about it, Penny. I know it would be a great opportunity to see if I could stand on my own and to be with Libby and her family, too. On the other hand, I hate to abandon you after you've done so much for me."

"Oh, Corbin. It is a great opportunity, and I don't think you should give it up. It will give you the experience of working with different groups of people and with the Haida culture. Our world is becoming much more diverse, and that job would prepare you better for more diverse students' needs. Having Libby's family there is icing on the cake. You definitely need to apply for it. I'll write you a wonderful recommendation; you will be a wonderful asset to any school."

"Thanks, Penny. You're so understanding. I think that's what makes you so good in your position. You always seem to be able to walk in others' shoes, whether it's a student, a teacher, an administrator, or even a friend. I'll never forget what you've done for Libby and me."

"And I'll never forget all you've done for me with your expertise and assistance. I will definitely remember it when I retire. If you think you'd like to come back to the prairies then, I'll put in a good word for you."

With Corbin leaving, Penny wondered who on staff she could get to fill his valuable spot. At the moment, there really wasn't anyone. The first priority was advertising for someone to fill his math teaching position. Maybe with luck she'd get another Corbin, but she wasn't overly optimistic. She'd just have to take on more responsibility. Actually, she'd just be taking back everything she had done alone before Corbin came home to work with her. Could she do it?

She was having to take on more responsibility with her parents, too. Her mother hadn't been feeling well lately, and she coughed continuously. Penny had tried to get her to give up her lifelong habit of smoking. Although Maudie didn't smoke in Penny's presence, she continued in secret when her daughter wasn't around. It had been her escape from stress ever since she'd come to Canada as a war bride.

One evening when Penny was visiting her parents, they got reminiscing about when she was a baby, and they told her the story about J.D. and Billy pushing her and Sheryl up the hill in a carriage by the beach and accidentally letting it go at the top. While Will described the rough ride the carriage had taken down the hill with the two young boys running after it, Maudie started laughing, which turned into coughing. She suddenly bent over in her chair, holding her chest in pain.

Penny jumped up from her chair, ran to her mother on the couch, and sat down beside her. Putting her arm around her, she said, "Mum, are you okay? Is it your heart?" Maudie attempted to clear her throat of phlegm, while continuing to cough. Suddenly she spit out rust-coloured sputum.

Realizing the colour was probably caused by blood in the phlegm, Penny called out to Will, who was sitting in his own La-Z-Boy, oblivious to what was happening. "Dad, we've got to get Mum to the hospital! Something's not right with her."

Will helped Penny get Maudie out to the car and sat with her in the back seat while Penny drove them to the hospital. Penny had been worried about her dad lately as well because he seemed to be out of it occasionally. Right now, Mum was the priority.

Maudie was admitted immediately, and Dr. Stanley, who had become head of the medical staff, began a series of tests. He forewarned Penny and Will of his suspicions. "From the description of her symptoms, and knowing of Mrs. Ryan's longtime smoking habit, we may be looking at lung cancer. Have you noticed any other changes in her health or activity lately?"

Will immediately spoke up. "She has seemed a little weak lately. Maudie has always zipped around the house keeping everything in order. Lately, it seems to make her breathe heavily, and she plops down on the couch for a rest. That's just not like her. I've been thinking about getting a housekeeper. Maybe if she'd eat more, she'd have more energy. She seems to have lost her appetite."

"Dad! Why haven't you told me these things?" Penny burst out, frowning with concern.

"You're so busy with your work, I didn't want to bother you."

Dr. Stanley broke into their exchange, trying to calm them down. "What's important today is finding out what your mother's problem is and doing the best we can to help her. If you two stay calm and support one another as you support Mrs. Ryan, that will work best for her."

Nodding her head in agreement, Penny slipped her arm around her father's waist and hugged him sideways. He responded by putting his arm around her shoulder and hugging her back.

The results were as Dr. Stanley had predicted. Maudie did have lung cancer; unfortunately, it had already begun to metastasize, and the prognosis was grim. The doctor recommended her going into the Health Science Cancer Center in Winnipeg, but Maudie refused to go. She wanted to remain in her home for the last days of her life.

This happened during the last days of the school year. Fortunately, Corbin was not leaving for Masset until the summer, so he took over Penny's responsibilities so she could be with her parents in their home.

A hospital bed was brought into the Ryan home, and hospice staff checked on Maudie every day and remained on call. Penny's nursing friend, Marylynn, also stopped by frequently to support

Penny as she cared for her parents. Understandably, Will was not handling the situation well.

One day as Penny was sitting by her mother's bedside, holding her hand, Maudie suddenly aroused, becoming more alert than usual. Slightly squeezing Penny's hand, she said, "I'm worried about your father, Penny. I don't think he's well. Promise me you'll look after him."

Startled by Maudie's sudden arousal and surprised at her request, Penny pulled herself together and replied, "Of course, Mum. You don't have to worry about me and Dad." She leaned over and kissed her mother on her forehead.

It was as if Penny's response gave Maudie permission to leave them. With a slight smile on her face, Maudie closed her eyes and drifted off to the next world.

Chapter
TWENTY-ONE

*O*ver the summer, Penny began to realize why her mother had asked her to take care of her father. She noticed that he was starting to repeat himself and that he couldn't remember details like where his tax papers were. Penny hadn't noticed the changes earlier because Maudie must have been covering for him.

As the summer months progressed, more changes surfaced. His sleep patterns had changed. He seemed more depressed, and although he always recognized Penny, other acquaintances he'd known in town for years became strangers to him. She began to worry if he was able to feed himself. Even more importantly, would he remember to shut off the stove when it wasn't in use? She decided to move back across the road to her once family home to watch over him.

Finally, Penny went with him to an appointment she'd made with Dr. Stanley. After checking Will's vital signs and asking a few questions that tested Will's cognitive abilities, he asked to speak with Penny alone.

"I'm afraid, Penny, your father is showing signs of early to moderate stages of Alzheimer's. I know your mother was starting to worry about him before she contracted her own terminal disease. I think it's progressing enough that he cannot be alone; he needs personal care. I know you're a busy woman, so you might consider looking into the Jackfish Senior Center here in Crocus

Plains. That way you can still see him as often as you can but you'll know that he is being cared for in the meantime."

Penny sucked in her breath and let it out again. This sudden news about her father's situation and additional responsibility in her own life was a shock. "I don't know if he will agree to that. Oh, I wish Corbin were still here to take over for me so I could give Dad the care he needs. He's already on the Queen Charlotte Islands getting ready for the opening of school there in his new position as principal. What will I do?" That wasn't a question meant for Dr. Stanley. Penny was just asking herself, but he responded anyway.

"You're a smart woman, and you love your father," said Dr. Stanley. "You will work out what's best for you both."

Thanking him for his confidence in her, she went into the reception area, where Will was waiting for her to take him home. Her first step was to move completely into the house with him. She had hired a new math teacher who was looking for a rental place, so she would offer her own place to her. Next, she would look into the senior center to see if there were openings for a resident. Then she'd begin having casual discussions with her father about his illness. She'd make gentle suggestions that the senior center would be a good choice for his care since she had too much responsibility at the collegiate to be able to give him the care he needed.

He seemed to be somewhat open to the idea during their conversations, even though he didn't often remember them later and would ask, "Who the hell's idea was that?"

Unfortunately, when she went to visit the Jackfish Senior Center, it was completely full; they weren't expecting any vacancies in the near future, and they had a waiting list of ten people ahead of Will. What would she do now? Some towns had caregiver groups that provided in-home care, but Crocus Plains was not one of those towns. When she called Dr. Stanley to let him know her situation, he suggested she look into the personal care homes in Brandon, which would be close enough for her to visit her dad on weekends while relieving her of the responsibility of his care.

While she had mixed feelings about the idea, she felt she had no choice. Not only did she have a huge responsibility at the school until they could replace her, but she also felt her own background was not sufficient to give him the care he needed. After lots of research and phone calls, she got him into a facility in Brandon.

As she packed up his belongings, they had conversations about what was happening. Sometimes Will was okay with the plan, sometimes he'd forget the plan, and sometimes he was a little angry about the plan.

On Labour Day weekend when Penny would normally be preparing for the opening day of school, they made the move to his place in Brandon. She stayed at a hotel one night so she could help settle him in and get used to being there as best she could in such a short time. The staff members were great; they were always checking on him, bringing him snacks, and making sure he went for his meals. During each of these times, they would have a little chat, and he started to tease them. When she left for home, Penny had good and sad feelings. She hated to leave him, but she felt confident that she'd made the best decision.

* * *

Penny was soon deep into the school year. She was getting to know her new staff member, who was also her neighbour since she was renting her little white clapboard house. Her name was Rhonda Masters, and a master she was.

Penny soon came to recognize that Rhonda was a female Corbin. She was an excellent math teacher, and the students loved her. Penny also discovered that Rhonda had already started taking administration courses, so she was able to pick up many of the responsibilities Corbin had done for Penny. Penny had a reputation of being one of the best in her field, so Rhonda had wanted to work under her for experience with an exceptional role model while she completed her courses and sought a position of her own.

As the school year progressed, Penny made day trips to Brandon on as many weekends as she could to take her dad for a ride to a park or for a meal at a restaurant if he was up for it. On days when he wasn't feeling so well, they would visit in his room. As Rhonda took on more responsibility, Penny felt that if she suddenly was called in to Brandon for an emergency, she could confidently leave the school in Rhonda's hands. She began to think retirement might not be too far off in her future.

One day, she did receive an urgent call, but it wasn't from the personal care home; it was from Will. He begged her to come and get him and bring him out to Crocus Plains to visit the cemetery. After checking with the supervisor to see if he were up for it, Penny was told that a day trip would probably be okay, especially since it would be to his hometown, where his original doctor was still available. She was also informed, however, that some of the physical symptoms of her dad's Alzheimer's were surfacing, such as issues with his bowels.

"Okay," Penny said. "Thanks for the information. I'll be sure we stop frequently. Please tell my dad that I will be in on Saturday to take him on his day trip." Then, laughing, she added, "You may have to remind him every day."

* * *

She left at six o'clock that Saturday morning so they'd have lots of time to get back to Crocus Plains to visit the cemetery and other places in town he might want to see. Maybe they could even drive out to the farm where he'd grown up. Starting early, they'd have time to work in both lunch and supper and still get him back to Brandon for bedtime.

Finally, they arrived at the cemetery, where oak, maple, and ash trees surrounded the perimeter. It was early June, so the snow was gone, but there was still a light spring breeze. The recently blossomed new foliage on the trees danced in the light breeze.

She had assumed that his request to come to the cemetery in Crocus Plains had been to visit her mother's grave. Where they stood, however, was not in the section where Maudie's grave lay, yet her father seemed visibly moved by whatever he was seeing and remembering. In fact, he had stooped so low that he was now kneeling before the tombstone.

Penny shifted so that she could see the headstone more clearly. Her mouth fell open as she read the name engraved in the granite: "Grace (Harris) Ryan, 1920–1942, Beloved wife of William Thomas Ryan." This must have been her father's first wife.

Will raised his tear-streaked face to look at Penny. As he moved, she could see that something else was written on the tombstone: "Baby Boy Ryan."

Penny's mouth dropped open again in surprise. Although she had always known that his first wife Grace had died in childbirth, she had not known that the baby had been a boy. What man doesn't want a son? Was that loss a part of his sadness?

Rising to his feet unsteadily, Will said, "I'm sorry, Penny. I guess I'm reliving the past today. I've always wondered what my son would have been like and what kind of a father I would have been to him."

"I'm sure you would have been great. Think about all the little boys who looked up to you, like Billy."

"Yes. I guess I was a good father to Billy."

Penny's eyes popped open, and she sucked in her breath. Will smiled as he continued, saying, "A good godfather, that is. I always wished I had a little guy like him."

"And he was your namesake, too," Penny reminded him, while thinking to herself, *He doesn't know. I wish I could tell him that he did have a son, and it was Billy. But I promised everyone I would never tell him or Billy.*

"Well, let's go see your mother," Will said as he took Penny's arm. Walking toward Maudie's grave, he continued, "Your mother saved me and became the love of my life. She also gave me the greatest gift a man could have: a wonderful daughter."

In front of Maude Ryan's tombstone, Will and Penny fell into one another's arms, sobbing. Regaining some composure, Will looked toward the tombstone, saying, "I'm here Maudie, with our girl. I love you with all my heart. I'll see you soon."

"Daddy, what do you mean?" Penny asked tearfully as Will grabbed her arm and started walking toward her car.

"I think you know what I mean, sweet pea. My time is coming. I wanted to come to the cemetery to say goodbye."

"Don't say that, Dad! You can't leave me," Penny responded, choking on her words.

But Will's premonition was right on. Two weeks later, Penny was back at the Crocus Plains Cemetery, saying goodbye to her father.

What will I do now? Penny wondered. She had just turned in her resignation as principal, retiring in order to spend more time with her dad. *Should I see if I can get my job back? Do I want to stay in Crocus Plains? There's no one here anymore who means anything to me.*

CHAPTER
TWENTY-TWO

*M*eanwhile on Haida Gwaii, the former Queen Charlotte Islands off the northwest coast of Canada, the group of friends who had formed a family crossing generations and cultures had gathered together to celebrate Corbin and Willow's engagement.

"Isn't this cool, Connor?" Libby said, turning to her husband. "With your sister marrying my brother, we've doubled our 'in-law' relationship with them."

"I guess you're right, Libby," Connor chuckled. "Have you guys made any wedding plans yet?" he asked Corbin.

Corbin responded, "We're thinking about having the ceremony out on the beach on the Tlell River in front of the lodge you built Connor. It's the same place where Sheryl and Deacon got married."

"That would be great!" Sheryl broke in. "We'd love to host your special day at our place." Sheryl and Deacon had bought Connor's lodge after he and Libby married and bought a former PMQ in Masset.

"Thanks, Sheryl," Corbin replied, then, turning to his sister, said, "You know who I'd like to have come to the wedding?"

"No, who? It's too bad the folks can't come, but they planned that trip back to the British Isles for years to see where their ancestors originated. Anyway, did you have someone else special in mind?" Libby asked.

"Penny. She played a big role in our lives in Crocus Plains. She was our summer nanny when we were little, and as the principal in the collegiate, she mentored me and encouraged me to become a principal myself."

"What a great idea!" Libby replied excitedly. "She mentored me, too, when I began teaching, and she was there for me when I lost Ben. We've been out of touch lately. She must be retired by now, right?"

Eyebrows pulled together quizzically, Sheryl asked, "Who is Penny? Should I know her?" It wasn't long ago that Sheryl, Libby, and Corbin had discovered that they had all originally come from Crocus Plains.

"Maybe," Corbin replied. "You're about the same age. Her last name is Ryan. Her dad was Will Ryan. I heard he passed away recently."

"Oh my God!" Sheryl gasped. "Penny and I grew up together. We were best friends from toddlers through high school. We went to different universities, but we taught one year together in Crocus Plains. We lost track of one another after I left for the Queen Charlotte Islands. Why didn't you two tell me you knew Penny?"

"Well, Sheryl, it hasn't been that long since we found out who you really were and where you came from. Until then, you were always Dr. Shirlee, ex-professor from the United States who became a coffee shop owner," Libby explained.

"All the more reason to invite Penny. I'm going to call her tonight," Corbin interjected.

"Tell her she can stay at our place," Libby and Sheryl said simultaneously.

* * *

Later that evening, the phone rang as Penny sat in her rocking chair, tearfully reflecting on memories of her parents and wondering what her future might bring. Sighing, she picked up the receiver and quietly said, "Hello?"

"Hi, Penny. It's me, Corbin."

"What a surprise! How are you?"

"I'm great, but how are you? I heard your dad passed away."

"Yes." Penny sighed again. "It's still hard, but he was ready, and he's now with his loves in heaven. So, what's up?"

"Well, Penny, my timing isn't great, but I have some wonderful news." Corbin hesitated, then continued. "I'm getting married to Willow."

"Oh my, that's wonderful. But who's Willow?' Penny asked.

"Remember when Libby and Connor came to Crocus Plains to get married and his half- sister flew out for the wedding? That was Willow Shaw."

"Oh, Corbin. She was beautiful. Didn't Libby think she was a Haida princess?"

Corbin chuckled. "Yes, she did. Anyway, we want you to come out for the wedding. And an old friend of yours wants you to come, too."

"I don't know anyone on the islands except you and Libby."

"Well, you apparently grew up in Crocus Plains with Sheryl Cross."

"Sheryl Cross? I never heard of her."

"Oh, sorry. That's her married name. She was Sheryl Leigh."

Penny bombarded him with questions. "You're kidding! What's she doing out there? Who's this Cross she married? Why didn't you or Libby tell me she was there earlier?"

Laughing, Corbin replied, "First of all, it hasn't been that long that we've known her real name and that she came from Crocus Plains. She was always Dr. Shirlee, owner of Dr. Shirlee's Books 'n' Brew, to us. I think we mentioned Dr. Shirlee to you at some point because she reminded us a lot of you. She has an education background, and she mentored both Libby and I. Oh, and she married Deacon Cross, the former NHL hockey player."

"What?!" Penny shouted. "How did she get back with him?"

"Oh, that's quite a story, and she'd love to tell it to you. Both she and Libby want you to stay with them. Will you come?"

"How can I not? I can't believe all this news! I've retired, Corbin, and I've been wondering what to do with myself. The answer just fell into my lap."

"Great!" Corbin said. Penny could hear the smile in his voice. "We'll be in touch with details and instructions for how to get here."

"Do I have to fly on that little plane from Prince Rupert Libby told me about?"

"No, Penny. You can now fly right into Masset from Vancouver on a turbojet. We'll be in touch. Goodnight."

"Goodnight," Penny replied, hanging up the phone. She sat back in her rocking chair, reflecting on what had just happened. *This is unbelievable! One moment I've lost my whole world, and the next a whole new world has opened up to me.*

* * *

On one of the last days of school in June, Penny talked with Rhonda, explaining the phone call she'd received from Corbin and sharing her plan for the summer. She asked Rhonda if she would keep an eye on her house while she was gone. She also told her that after she'd submitted her resignation earlier in the month, she had also submitted a recommendation for Rhonda to take her place. "I used to think, Rhonda, that you were my female Corbin. Now I think you are just me."

"That's quite a compliment, Penny. Of course I'll watch the house, and thank you for the reference. I would love to be the principal here, but you will be a tough act to follow."

"You'll do a great job, and your education is more recent, so you have more up-to-date ideas to incorporate. If I can be of any help, don't be afraid to call on me if you need to discuss anything."

"Thanks, Penny. I am so glad that this new adventure with old friends has surfaced. You've had such a tough couple of years with losing your folks. I hope this opens up a whole new future for you."

"Thanks, Rhonda. I appreciate your good wishes, and I hope your new position turns out to be a wonderful new future for you, too."

Penny had a couple of surprises in the next couple of days. First of all, a brief letter came in the mail from Corbin, including two plane tickets. One was for July 1 from Winnipeg to Vancouver on Air Canada, then from Vancouver to Masset on Pacific Coastal. In his letter, he explained that they were only one-way tickets because he wanted her to stay as long as she wanted. The wedding was scheduled for July 7. He also told her to be sure she toured the Vancouver airport to see some of the Haida art, especially *Spirit of Haida Gwaii*, a jade canoe sculpture created by Bill Reid, one of the artists who inspired the renaissance of Haida art.

The second surprise was a phone call from her longtime lost friend, Sheryl (Leigh) Cross. "Hi, Penny. How are you, girlfriend?" asked Sheryl.

"Thrilled to hear from you. After all these years, I can't believe we're in touch again. I don't know what happened that we lost one another. And how did you end up with Deacon again?"

"First of all, I'm sorry we lost touch. I guess I have to take responsibility for that. There was no way you could have followed my whereabouts, but I should have written you. After all, you stayed in the same place."

"True, I didn't leave, but how could you have known that either? Your parents were gone, and J.D. was all over the world and had no reason to come back either, so I had no way of finding out where you were. Where have you been, and how did you get on those remote islands?"

"Well, first of all," began Sheryl, "you remember after my folks had both died and I had no real reason to stay in Crocus Plains, I decided to go for my master's back at the University of North Dakota. I enjoyed working with the students so much as a GTA, I went on for my PhD in education and eventually became a professor of teacher education.

"Do you remember my old roommate, Tiffany? She's the one who had asked me to be her maid of honour when she married Rob Black, Deacon's buddy on the UND Fighting Sioux hockey team. They ended up in Denver with twin girls, and I visited them often. While I was a professor, I got an urgent call from Rob saying Tiff had died of ovarian cancer. I went out to the funeral, and while I was there, her girls found a letter in her personal stuff that Deacon had written to me. Remember how I thought he'd abandoned me? Well, that idea was reinforced by Tiffany's comments that a high-profile hockey player wouldn't be interested in me when he had women all over him. Well, while I was at home when Dad had his heart attack, that letter from Deacon arrived at our dorm. He had sent me a plane ticket to Vancouver so we could plan our life together, and in the letter he as much as asked me to marry him. Jealousy must have been the reason that Tiff never gave me the letter. Rob also confirmed that Deacon had called me but Tiff told him I was in Manitoba and wasn't interested anymore. I found out in my middle age that she had betrayed me and that's how Deacon and I had lost one another.

"Finding this out made me feel like I'd lost him all over again, and I found it difficult to stay at UND where our love had begun. I remembered visiting the Charlottes to see J.D. and his family after graduation when I'd lost Deacon the first time—or thought I had—and decided that might be a great place to escape to. They needed a coffee shop, and I thought it would be a peaceful environment to write the great American or Canadian novel, although I never did do that. So that's how I ended up here."

"Wow. That's quite a story. I'm so sorry Tiff was so heartless. But how did you and Deacon finally get together?"

"Deacon had played with the Vancouver Canucks; then in his retirement he became their marketing manager. The team made a trip to the islands to meet their fans while on a team-building retreat, and Deacon came into my coffee shop. He was upset that I'd ignored his letter, and I explained to him how that had happened. As we talked about our past, we could still feel the attraction between us, and we decided it's never too late in life to find love. What about you, Penny? I understand you've never married."

"I'm so happy for you and Deacon. I guess I've had my troubles with love, and now I'm too old to find it."

"Don't say that, girlfriend. I proved it's never too late. You can tell me your stories when you come up in July."

"Yes, I'll share them with you, but I don't think there are any happy endings for me. Where would I find love now?"

"Never say never. And you're coming to the islands. Who knows where love might find you? Anyway, I can hardly wait to see you and get caught up. I've missed you so much over the years. Until then, take care, Penny."

"You, too, Sheryl. See you soon."

CHAPTER
TWENTY-THREE

*I*t was July 1, Canada Day, which was a busy day for travel, but Penny was on the final leg of her journey. The Pacific Coastal turbojet flew up the British Columbia coast and circled over the Hecate Strait. From her seat, Penny could see a sandbar where sea lions were playing, then a circular fenced-in military station someone on the plane referred to as the Elephant Cage. Finally, the plane approached the paved runway, landed smoothly, and taxied up to the new airport terminal at Masset. She could see Corbin and Libby waiting outside for her.

Greeting her with hugs, they both welcomed her to the islands and led her into the building to get her bags. While waiting for them to arrive, Libby explained, "I get to have you first tonight, Penny. Sheryl and I had a little fight over it." Seeing Penny's frown, she laughed and added, "Just kidding. Since you've had a long day already, we decided it would be best if you stayed in town with us tonight, then Sheryl and Deacon will come in to Masset tomorrow to take you back to their place on the Tlell River. We know you two have a lot of years to catch up on."

Arriving at Libby's house, a former PMQ, Penny recognized Aimée Parker on the front step outside the house next door. She was waving at the car. Penny remembered Libby saying they'd been friends and then neighbours when the military sold their housing to locals.

"Aimée knew you were coming up; she remembers you from our wedding back in Crocus Plains," said Libby. Watching Aimée go back inside, she added, "She wanted to greet you, but she can't come over as she's got four kids at home and Stephen's at work. We'll get a chance to visit one day."

"What about your kids? Isn't Connor at work, too?" asked Penny.

"Yes, he is. But Willow's taken some time off work to plan the wedding, so her assistant is looking after Raven's Nook, her Haida art and gift shop. She said she would stay with Zach and Bella for me while we picked you up."

Penny enjoyed her evening with the Fergusons, getting to know Connor more, playing a few games with Zach, and reading a bedtime story to little Bella. She also got feedback on Corbin's first year as principal on the islands and got to know Willow, his bride-to-be. After having a final evening chat with Libby over crackers, cheese, and a glass wine, she collapsed in their guest room, falling asleep quickly after such a long day.

She was having a morning cup of coffee and a bran muffin with Libby when a knock came at the door around nine o'clock. Grinning, Libby suggested, "Would you get that for me?"

Thinking the request was a little odd, Penny obliged and opened the door. A woman about her age with faded blond hair and silver highlights greeted her, "Penny! I can't believe you're here!" and reached out to hug her.

Hugging her back, Penny grinned and asked, "Sheryl, is that really you? You're beautiful. You've aged well." Looking behind her at a tall handsome man with silver hair, she added, "And you must be Deacon. I'm so pleased to meet you. I hope you're treating my girlfriend well."

Deacon reached out to shake Penny's hand and said, laughing, "Sheryl warned me you were a joker."

"Well, to a point," Penny said with a serious tone. "But I have always wanted the best for Sheryl." When she saw a confused look come across Deacon's face, she grinned again and said, "I'm just teasing. From what I understand, you are the best, and I'm so happy for you both."

"Glad you said that," said Deacon, "or I'd be leaving you here instead of bringing you to our place." When Sheryl nudged him with her elbow, he laughed and added, "See? I can tease, too."

Penny gathered up her things, Deacon loaded them in his Jeep, and they left Libby's place. Before leaving town, they drove down the main street to show Penny Dr. Shirlee's Books 'n' Brew, Sheryl's coffee shop and secondhand book store.

"Why aren't you at work today, Sheryl? I don't want to keep you from your routine."

"Not a problem, Penny. Carla, who worked for me as a teen-ager, has stayed on the islands and occasionally runs the place for me. We live a distance from town, and I'm actually thinking about retiring. Libby and Aimée have thought about taking it over, especially now that their kids are getting older and will soon all be in school. They could always come there after school was done for the day and do homework until their mothers close up.

"There are a lot more shops, restaurants, hotels, and bed-and-breakfast places established since I first came here," she continued. "When the military stood down in the mid-1990s, the locals and the Haida First Nation had to establish other means of economic development, and they have done a fantastic job. There is even a new coffee shop in town, so we could just close up and sell the building for some other entrepreneurial investment. There are lots of other things we can do to keep us busy, not that we need to. But both Deacon and I have enjoyed teaching classes at the college."

"Sounds like you've created quite a wonderful life for yourselves. As I said earlier, I am so happy for you both."

By this time, they were well on their way down Highway 16. "By the way, aren't you hosting the wedding and reception?" Penny asked. "I hope I can help you with anything you might need."

"Actually," said Sheryl, "there's been a change in plans. Willow and Corbin decided it would be better to have it located more centrally since they know a lot of people and it wouldn't be as private a wedding as Deacon's and mine. Willow has attended St. John's Anglican Church out in Old Masset for several years, so they would like the ceremony there. There has also been a community center built out there in recent years, and they are going to get one of the restaurants to cater the reception there. So I guess we can just relax and enjoy the celebration as guests. We are going to have a little family gathering the week following the wedding at our lodge."

"Do you both have family up here?" Penny asked.

Sheryl laughed and explained, "Not a biological family; our friends, young and old, have developed such a close relationship over the years that we have become a kind of family."

"Sounds wonderful," Penny responded.

"Speaking of family, I was really sorry to hear of your mother and father's passing. They were such great people. Our families were almost like relatives, too."

"Thanks, Sheryl," Penny said. "I do miss them, but I was fortunate in that I had them a lot longer than you had yours. Your folks were great, too. Remember all those fun times we had at your lake cabin?"

"Ah, yes. They were great times." At that moment, Deacon pulled the car up next to a beautiful red cedar lodge surrounded by tall cedar and spruce trees. They got out of the car and walked to the front of the lodge, which was encircled by an inviting veranda stocked with comfortable log rocking chairs and benches.

"I can understand why you love it here. It's so peaceful and beautiful," Penny commented, looking from the veranda out to the river and beach.

"Yes, we were lucky to get it when Connor decided that the family should live in town so he would be closer to work and Zach would be closer to school when he started. Of course, now there's Bella, too. It's nice for them to be next door to the Parkers, too. Come on in. Let's get you settled in." Sheryl showed Penny to their guest room and helped her unpack.

After lunch, Deacon went out to fish in the Tlell River, hoping to get a salmon or steelhead for supper. Sheryl and Penny sat for a while longer at the table, sipping on their tea and catching up on their lives and others' stories.

Sheryl plied her with questions. "What about Bernie and Roger? Did they get back safely from Vietnam? Where are they now? Did Roger go into engineering? I always thought Bernie might end up in politics. What about him?"

"Yes, they got back in one piece from Vietnam, but it was a horrific experience. They can't stand to hear fireworks or a car backfire; it reminds them of explosions. Actually, they both ended up back in Crocus Plains in business. They took over their fathers' stores. Bernie is in the bakery, and he renamed it Bernie's Bakery. Roger took over his dad's hardware store, and with his love of fishing, he renamed his store Jackfish Hardware."

"Did I ever tell you that in North Dakota I learned that Americans call jackfish 'northern pike' and pickerel 'walleye'? That's just tidbit of information. Did our old buddies ever find women in their lives?"

"No, you hadn't told me about the fish names, but yes, they married some great gals, a hairdresser and a nurse. That's probably one of the reasons they stayed in Crocus Plains."

"What about Diane and Marsy, our friends from high school?"

"They were both at Brandon University at the same time I was," said Penny. "In fact, they were in the dorm room next to Ginny and me. They went to Winnipeg and got jobs at Red River College. I think one was in the library and the other in marketing. I can't quite remember as we lost touch, but I did hear they both married guys who also worked in the college and settled in Transcona, a suburb of the city."

"You mentioned your roommate Ginny. What about her?" Sheryl asked.

"Well, she went on for her master's in English and did her thesis about Margaret Laurence, that famous Canadian author who was also from Neepawa. Ginny's studies inspired her to become a writer herself. I think she married an American and lives in the US now."

Taking a sip from her teacup, Penny suddenly felt a thick hand on her shoulder as a male voice said, "Hello, Sis!"

Choking on her tea, Penny turned and looked up toward the voice. Sandy hair striped with grey crowned familiar blue eyes looking down at her. "Billy! Is that you?" Penny cried out.

"Yes, it is. Got a hug for your brother?"

Stunned, Penny pulled herself out of her chair and into Billy's arms, asking, "Why did you call me 'Sis'? And yourself my brother?"

"Penny, you know darn well why I did. You're the one who broke us up because of it."

"How did you find out?"

Sheryl broke in, saying, "I have to confess, Penny, I told my brother J.D. the secret long ago. When Billy was with us one weekend years later, he was still so depressed about losing you, and he couldn't understand why you had broken it off. J.D. thought I had to tell him the truth."

"I understood your rejection then, Penny, but J.D. and I started to wonder if maybe Nora had made a mistake. There was no way of proving it back in those days, but now DNA testing can determine fatherhood. It was, of course, easy to get my sample, but getting your dad's was a challenge. He was in that personal care home in Brandon by then, so we went to visit him. I had always felt close to Will, so I wanted to visit him anyway even if we couldn't get a sample. We remembered he liked rum and Coke, so we took him a glass and made him a drink. When we left, we took the glass, too, and found a lab to do the test. Sure enough, Penny, you're my half-sister. We share a dad."

"Oh, Billy, I've thought of you so often, wishing I hadn't had to hurt you. A few times I also wondered if Nora might have been wrong. Have you had a happy life? I've prayed that you have."

"Yes, Penny. There was never going to be anyone like you, but I did find a woman that I could love, and we had a family together. In fact, we're going to be grandparents."

Penny threw herself into his arms, crying, "Oh, Billy! I'm so glad. These are tears of happiness. How did you happen to be here?"

"Sheryl told me you were coming for Corbin's wedding, so I decided to make a run up to see you and let you know that I know the whole story. I wanted us to reconnect and live our lives without such discomfort and worry about each other. Betsy and I live in Victoria now, so it was a quick flight up, and I'm going back tomorrow."

Sheryl added, "He'll stay for supper with us this evening so you two can have some more time to catch up, and then Deacon will drive him back to Masset to his hotel so he'll be ready to catch his early flight in the morning. Why don't you go relax on the veranda and talk? I'll bring some coffee."

They followed Sheryl's suggestion, and once they were settled in, Billy wanted to know about Penny's love life. She, of course, had no happy news to share with him. Her love life had been a disaster, and his shoulders sank in despair when she shared her stories. "I used to look out for you in high school; I wanted to protect you. I wish I'd been there for you as your brother. You're still beautiful, Penny. It's never too late to find love. Maybe it's still out there waiting for your discovery."

"Oh, you sound like Sheryl. I know it worked for her, but I'm not getting my hopes up. Maybe I don't even want to go through all that again at my age."

Billy reached for her hand and said, "I'll be keeping you in my thoughts and heart and hoping your life is wonderful regardless of what the future holds."

Squeezing his hand and smiling at him with love and gratitude shining in her eyes, she said, "Thank you, Brother."

CHAPTER
TWENTY-FOUR

The next morning, Sheryl woke Penny up to tell her she and Deacon had to go in to Masset to open up the coffee shop because Carla, her assistant, had to take her mother to the doctor. "We both know what that's like," she said to Penny. "Anyway, you can stay here and relax. I just wanted you to know what was up so you didn't wonder where we were when you got up."

"Oh, I want to come with you. I can be ready in five minutes. I'd love to see inside your shop, and maybe I can help you," Penny responded, climbing out of bed and grabbing her housecoat to head to the bathroom.

"If you're sure you want to come. You don't have to help. You might want to wander around downtown to see some of the changes I told you about, or there's plenty of secondhand books to choose from if you'd like to just sit, read, and drink coffee."

"Sounds like a fun day," Penny called out from the bathroom.

As she'd said, Penny was ready in five minutes, and soon they were on their way to town. As they approached the main street, Penny smiled as she saw the window of the shop adorned with the name in bright red gothic lettering, Dr. Shirlee's Books 'n' Brew.

"Where'd you get that name for your coffee shop? I get the 'Books 'n' Brew' part, but what about Dr. Shirlee?"

"Do you remember that old Dolly Parton movie *Straight Talk*? Well, in the movie, she adopted the name Dr. Shirlee when she filled in for an advice talk show on the radio. Guess it was a way of remembering my own background as a PhD."

"Yes, and she's always full of advice," added Deacon, laughing.

"How well I remember," Penny agreed. Then, remembering their talk about love the day before, she laughed and added, "Still is!"

Entering the shop, Penny was impressed with the setup. The coffee counter was immediately inside the shop to the left of the entrance. Full shelves of books extended from the counter and along the back wall. Overstuffed chairs were scattered in front of shelves for comfortable reading. The rest of the room was filled with tables covered in red-and-white checkered cloths that matched the gingham curtains on the windows.

While Penny scanned the bookshelves, Sheryl got the coffee going. Soon Penny could smell the spicy aroma of flavoured coffee. "Oh, Sheryl, that smells yummy. What would you recommend? I'm going to take this book over to that table in the back corner by the window to read and sip coffee."

"Well, Penny since you picked Libby's favourite spot from when she first came to the islands to teach, I'll make you her favourite latte, an almond roca mocha."

"Sounds yummy. Where's Deacon?"

"Oh, he went to see if Rob wants to come over for coffee since we're in town today."

"Rob? Who's that? Am I supposed to know him?" Penny asked.

"Oh, sorry, Penny. You've heard of him, but you've never met him. It's Rob Black, Deacon's hockey buddy from UND, and Tiffany's husband."

"What's he doing here? How can you stand to be around him after what Tiffany did to you and Deacon?"

"First of all, Rob's a good guy. He didn't know what Tiffany was up to, and he was madly in love with her. Sometimes we really don't know another person. I think you found that out, too, from the story you told me about Rodney." Penny nodded her head in agreement as Sheryl continued. "Actually, Rob found another letter from Tiff she'd written for me after she realized she was dying. In it she confessed what she'd done and asked for forgiveness. I received it on the day Deacon and I got married. As Willow helped me understand that day, it gave me a release from all the bitterness I had held inside, and her letter became a blessing on our second chance at love."

"Oh, Sheryl, you've been through so much. But now why is he up here?"

"Rob retired from coaching the Denver Pioneers a few years ago. He likes to spend time with his daughters, who live in other parts of the US, but he also likes to escape the Colorado winters, so he spends them down in Florida. He eventually bought a home there in an active adult community, but he can't stand the excessive heat and humidity during the summer, so Deacon invited him to come up and visit us. He kind of fell in love with the place, so for the rest of the summer, we're renting him the cottage I lived in before Deacon and I were married.

"It's a lovely little cedar cabin among the trees down by the bay. Actually, it's been home to many of us in our 'family.' Libby rented it from a retired military captain and his wife when she first came to the islands. They liked to spend their summers here, but they visited their children and grandchildren the rest of the year. When Libby married Connor and moved to the lodge he'd built out on the Tlell, I moved into the cabin, as it was a more appropriate size for me than one of the former PMQs. When the captain and his wife decided they wanted to spend more time with their family, they sold me the cabin. Then when Connor and Libby bought a PMQ and moved to town, Deacon and I bought Connor's lodge. In the meantime, Corbin had arrived to be the principal, so we rented the cabin to him. Now, of course, he's moved in with Willow in her house. So we have the cabin to use if we want to stay overnight in town, or we rent it out or loan it to friends. Here's your latte. Make yourself comfortable at Libby's table, and I'll bring you a scone shortly."

"This latte smells as yummy as it sounded. Thanks, Sheryl. Your cabin sounds delightful. I hope you can show it to me while I'm here."

Penny walked to the corner table. She had just settled in when the door opened, and in walked Deacon with presumably his friend Rob. He was shorter than Deacon and a little huskier, but he had light brown hair with less grey in it than Deacon. Sheryl made their favourite coffee drinks, and she promised to bring them scones in a few minutes as well.

Turning to find a table, Deacon spotted Penny and walked over to her. "Penny, this is my friend Rob, and Rob, this is Sheryl's longtime friend Penny from Crocus Plains, Manitoba. Mind if we join you, Penny?"

"Of course; pull up a chair." Grinning, Penny added, "Pleased to meet you, Rob. I've heard lots about you."

"Uh-oh. That doesn't sound good," Rob replied, laughing with a twinkle in his hazel eyes. "What can you tell me about her, Deacon?"

"Oh, you're both good, but you're also both teasers." Noting that more customers were starting to file in for their coffee breaks, Deacon said, "Oops, looks like I'd better go help my girl. Enjoy your coffee, folks."

Sitting down across from Penny, Rob said, "I guess you're stuck with me now. So, teaser, tell me about yourself. Do you have a husband and family waiting for you back in Manitoba?"

"Nope, I never married, so unfortunately I have no kids either. I've heard you have children and grandchildren." Holding back tears from the memory of her own loss, she said, "I'm sorry you lost your wife to cancer. That's tough to go through. I lost my mother to that horrible disease. Sheryl's always saying it's never too late to find love, so have you been able to let someone else into your life? Oh, sorry. We just met. That may be too personal to ask yet."

Rob laughed and said, "That's okay. I trust you since you're a good friend of Sheryl's. Actually, I was recently dating someone before coming up to the islands. Maybe it will develop more upon my return. You know, absence makes the heart grow fonder."

"Yeah, for somebody else!" Penny laughed, and Rob burst out laughing, too. "Sorry, again. That's a line my mother used to say."

"You're funny," Rob said. "How much of the town have you seen? I guess it's changed a lot since Sheryl first came to Masset and opened her shop."

"I arrived the day before yesterday. I stayed overnight with Libby, then went to Sheryl and Deacon's place yesterday on the Tlell, so I haven't been in town long enough to explore. How about you?"

"I've been here for a month already, and they've taken me on tours in Masset and Old Massett, the Haida First Nation village. I want to get down to Skidegate sometime, as they've developed a wonderful Haida Heritage Centre. Anyway, do you feel like going for a walk around the downtown area while they're busy? I can fill you in on what they told me."

"Sounds like a plan. Let's finish these wonderful scones and then go."

Fifteen minutes later, they told Sheryl and Deacon what their plan was and left the shop. Deacon and Sheryl looked at one another with eyebrows raised and at the same time said, "Interesting."

Rob first took her to the former military parade square. "It's just open space now, but it used to have an administration building over there to the right, then all the way across the square was the clinic and hospital. They were all torn down after the military pulled out."

"Don't they have any health care here now?" Penny asked.

"Yes, there's a new large regional medical facility out in Old Massett. We can take a drive out there another day to see those changes. Across the street from the parade square was the only hotel and restaurant here. It was called the Seegay Inn. It apparently burnt down in the '70s. Now there are many restaurants, hotels, and bed-and-breakfasts. We'll walk past some of them. There was also only one store, a co-op. There are others now, but even the co-op has expanded. A lot more produce and baked goods are available now than there were back in the day."

Strolling off the main street, Rob took Penny to see other additions that had surfaced after the military had left, including the Northwest Community College, Masset's Municipal Library, which was named after former teacher Jesse Simpson, and the Dixon Entrance Maritime Museum, where they spent a good hour learning about the history of the islands. Getting hungry, they continued down the street to Bud's Bar and Grille, a café that was modeled after the 1950s, and enjoyed a hamburger and fries for lunch.

After going to the inlet and walking out on the government wharf, they returned to the coffee shop, where Sheryl and Deacon were getting ready to close up.

"We'll drop you off at the cottage, Rob, then we'll head home," Deacon said as they walked to his Jeep.

When they arrived at the attractive little cedar cottage, Rob asked, "Would you folks like to come in for a glass of wine before you head home?" Sheryl noticed that his eyes were particularly on Penny as he invited them in, so she agreed for them all.

The outside of the cottage had been attractive, but Penny found the inside just as charming. The open space consisted of a small kitchenette in one corner to the left of the entrance, with the counters and appliances making an L-shape around the walls. A round table with four chairs sat in the center. Across the room was a stone fireplace with a worn brown leather couch and a matching recliner facing it. Haida-designed throws lay over the backs of the couch and chair. Alongside the fireplace was a small desk.

On the opposite side of the fireplace was the entrance to the bedroom, which was furnished with a bed, a dresser, and a rocking chair made of rough-hewn logs. A woven blanket bearing the Haida Raven and Eagle symbols was casually flung over the chair.

"This cottage is delightful, Sheryl, and so cozy. You must have loved staying here when you were on your own."

"Yes, Penny, I did, and I especially enjoyed relaxing on the porch at the back, which faces the harbor. Come and take a look while the guys are getting our wine." Sheryl led Penny out the back door, where two inviting willow rocking chairs were placed side by side facing the water. A worn path led to the dock, where a wooden rowboat was moored.

"I can certainly understand your being able to relax out here. It's so peaceful. One could lose herself here." Penny sighed.

"You're not the first one to say that," Sheryl replied, smiling. "I think the guys are ready for us."

Reentering the cottage, they found the guys already settled on the couch with their wine and a small plate of cheese slices. "Grab your glasses from the table, gals, and join us in front of the fire," Rob called to them. It had cooled off later in the day, so the open fire made the cottage cozy.

As they sat making plans to take Penny on tours of the islands, Deacon suggested they pack a picnic lunch to take out to Tow Hill; they could climb the hiking path, see the Blow Hole, and have their picnic on Agate Beach.

"I've forgotten, Deacon, are there bathroom facilities out there in case we need them?" Sheryl asked.

"Oh, don't worry, Sheryl," Deacon responded. "There's plenty of trees and shrubs around that can give us privacy if needed."

"Easy for you to say," Sheryl accused.

"Mum always used to say guys have a handy thing to take on a picnic." Penny grinned.

Deacon chuckled as Rob burst into laughter, saying, "You are so funny!"

Grinning, Sheryl said, "That does sound like Maudie."

They started to make plans for their adventure on the following weekend until they realized that was Corbin and Willow's wedding weekend. When they left for the evening, Rob walked them out to Deacon's Jeep. Walking alongside Deacon, he said, "That gal's so funny and nice. I think I want to spend some time with her." He stood on the front porch and waved goodbye as the Jeep left the area and made its way out to Highway 16, down to the Tlell River, and back to the Crosses' lodge.

As they got ready for bed, Deacon told Sheryl what Rob had said to him about Penny. "Too bad he isn't invited to the wedding this weekend," Deacon concluded.

Interested in getting Penny thinking about a relationship again, Sheryl replied, "I know he hasn't been here long and the bride and groom really don't know him, but I'm sure if I asked Corbin if he could come with us, he'd give us the okay."

Corbin did say, "Of course," when they asked, and they picked up Rob on the way to St. John's Anglican Church the next weekend. Pulling into a space on the street to park, Sheryl explained to Rob and Penny the significance of the beautifully carved totem pole in the church's yard. "In the past, many original totems were lost through weathering and sometimes were stolen. A renaissance of Haida art—and particularly the totem poles—began with this totem pole being carved and raised by Robert Davidson, a descendant of Charles Edenshaw, a notable carver in the golden age of Haida art at the turn of the twentieth century. The raising of Davidson's pole in 1969, was historic because it was the first totem raised on the islands in almost one hundred years."

"Totem carving must have really grown again since then," said Rob. "There are several here in Old Massett, and I understand the Haida Heritage Centre in Skidegate has a wonderful tour of the totems on display there. Penny, maybe you and I should go to visit the center and see them when Deacon and Sheryl are busy again at the shop."

Penny smiled and replied, "Sounds like a plan. But right now, it looks like we'd better get in the church or we'll miss the wedding, which is the whole reason I came to Haida Gwaii."

Rob perused Penny's attractive plum-coloured dress, which had sequined lace on the bodice and a chiffon-covered taffeta skirt that hit Penny mid-calf. He commented, "Maybe it won't be the only reason you stay for a while."

As they walked to the church entrance, Sheryl nudged Penny, who had ignored Rob's comment, and whispered, "I think someone is showing some interest in you. You really are beautiful, Penny. How have you been able to avoid going grey? Do you dye your hair?" Sheryl looked at Penny's reddish-highlighted brunette hair, which was the same as she remembered from their youth. It was styled in a smooth short pageboy cut that curled under loosely just below her jawline. The top was parted on the left side and flowed toward the right side.

"No, Sheryl. I don't dye my hair, and I never have. I'm lucky to have inherited my mother's hair. Even when she died, she still only had a few strands of grey in her hair."

"You have her beautiful warm brown eyes, too," Sheryl added as they entered the front door and walked into the sanctuary.

The service was a combination of Anglican service and Haida traditions. Corbin and Willow made a handsome couple, and Penny could tell their love was real and deep. She was so glad that both the little kids she'd nannied had found true love on the Misty Isles, the local nickname for Haida Gwaii, which meant "Islands of the People" in the Haida language. Would that ever happen for her? Probably much too late.

At the reception, Sheryl, who still had a strong voice that had developed even more depth with maturity, sang Cat Stevens' version of "Morning Has Broken," which Corbin had performed at her and Deacon's wedding. It was her blessing on their marriage. Neither the bride or groom had parents present, but Connor and Libby were their attendants, representing family and providing a wonderful example of true love.

A DJ supplied the music for a short dance. The bride and groom danced the first dance to "Amazed" by Lonestar. Connor and Libby joined them at the end. The DJ then stepped up the pace with some rock and roll and a polka. When Deacon and Sheryl joined the crowd, Rob looked at Penny and asked, "Do you know how to polka?"

"Of course. I'm a prairie girl," she said as she grinned.

"Well, come on, prairie girl, let's do it!" Rob grabbed her hand, dragged her onto the floor, and immediately jumped into the hopping one-two-three rhythm of "Roll Out the Barrel." They seemed to fall into step as if they'd danced together before, and they flew around the floor under the other guests' observation. At the end of the polka, they got a round of applause from the crowd.

When the DJ announced the last dance and began George Strait's "I Cross My Heart," Rob immediately drew Penny into his arms and glided with her around the floor, gradually pulling her closer until they were dancing cheek to cheek by the last few lines. This did not go unnoticed by Sheryl and Deacon.

At the end of the dance, the four hugged the bride and groom and wished them well before leaving. Penny also hugged

Libby, who having noticed the interaction between Penny and Rob, whispered in Penny's ear, "Are you sure you want to go back to Sheryl and Deacon's place? Maybe you have a reason to stay in town. You're always welcome at our place."

"Thanks, Libby, but I'd better go home with Sheryl tonight. I would like to have more time with you though, so maybe I'll spend a few days at your place before I go home."

* * *

When they dropped off Rob at the cottage before going back to the lodge, he told Penny he would come out to the lodge on Monday to pick her up so they could go down to the southern part of Graham Island to visit the Haida Heritage Centre and the Haida Gwaii Museum. Sheryl and Deacon would have to take over their shop's duties that day because Carla was still tied up with her mother's illness. It was making them think more about retirement and selling the coffee shop.

On Monday, the Crosses had already left for Masset when Rob arrived to pick up Penny. She was ready, and they took off down Highway 16.

"How far is it to the center?" Penny asked.

"From Masset, it's about 112 clicks, so from their place, it's probably around eighty clicks."

Penny laughed. "I'm surprised a Yankee like you would know to call kilometers 'clicks,' or for that matter even know the distance in kilometers rather than miles."

"I'm not a Yankee. I'm from Colorado," Rob said.

"Oh, to Canadians all Americans are Yankees," she laughed, then continued, "It was kind of ironic that Canada went to the metric system in the mid-1970s because the United States was planning to. When you live next door to a superpower, you want to cooperate with them. But the irony was that we did it and you Yankees didn't."

Laughing, Rob replied, "I guess we sucked you Canucks in again."

"Okay, let's call a truce. I won't call you a Yank anymore."

By then they'd reached the Heritage Center, which was a couple of kilometers south of Skidegate at Ḵay Llnagaay, meaning "sea lion town." The totem tour was to happen at eleven o'clock, so they toured the interior of the museum and center first, looking at all the Haida art on the walls and the notices explaining the cultural history of this proud and talented First Nation. There were also videos to watch for more information and a nice gift shop to get books and other souvenirs to remember the culture.

At eleven, they joined the crowd in front of the indoor totem to meet the guide and start the tour. A beautiful young Haida woman explained that the six totem poles along the front of the building had been assigned to specific carvers who had been commissioned to represent each of the six original villages in the southern part of the island. She then led the group outside and went to each totem pole, explaining the meaning of each carved part of the pole and the significance of certain symbols to the Haida culture. She explained that at the top of the totems were three circular tube shapes that were called the Three Watchmen. They represented the watchmen for each village, who observed water, sky, and land for any potential danger approaching the village.

The front of the center faced the water of the bay. After the tour, Rob and Penny walked around the yard, looking at the canoes painted in beautiful traditional Haida style. Inside a carving shed, they watched the process for carving a totem pole. The red cedar log being used was forty feet long and six hundred years old. The master carver had drawn the pattern on the pole, and he then supervised his interns in carving the designs. An older totem carved by Bill Reid that had fallen during a storm had also been brought to the shed to be preserved.

Hungry, they had lunch in Kay's Bistro, the center's lunchroom, which was also decorated with Haida art. Then they started their journey back to the lodge, discussing all they'd learned and appreciated about the Haida First Nation. As they got closer to the turnoff to the Crosses' lodge, Rob suggested that he take her into Masset instead. "The coffee shop won't be closing until at least four, so I might as well take you into town. Then maybe we can have dinner in town all together and you can go back to the lodge with Deacon and Sheryl."

"Okay," Penny agreed, thinking she didn't want to end the wonderful day yet anyway.

Pulling up to Dr. Shirlee's Books 'n' Brew, they immediately noticed the "Closed" sign. "What's going on?" Penny wondered.

"I don't know," Rob responded, "but we'd better find out. Let's go to the cottage and give them a call."

Rob called and found out that Deacon and Sheryl were at home. They'd closed up early because there hadn't been much business. "We're not the only coffee shop in town now," Deacon told Rob. "We don't have the huge following we used to. It's making Sheryl and I think even more that it may be time to sell the building to someone with a new business project. We're really thinking we're ready for retirement. We could travel more, and when we're home we can relax in our lodge as we enter the autumn of our lives."

"You might also consider spending time in the south during the winter months. There are lots of Canadians in my development," Rob suggested.

At Sheryl's urging, Deacon asked, "Is Penny still with you? Are you going to bring her out here?"

Looking at Penny, Rob said, "Well, we've had kind of a long, full day. We'd planned to go out for dinner with you folks before you all went home. If it's okay with her, I think she should just stay in town, and I can bring her home tomorrow or to the shop to go home with you."

Frowning with her head bent, Penny wondered how this would work. She felt that she couldn't expect Rob to drive her out or Deacon to come and get her after they'd all had such a busy day. Since she didn't say anything, Rob assumed his suggestion was okay with her, and he said goodbye to Deacon.

"Are you hungry, Penny? We can still go out to eat. There's Charter's Restaurant down by the marina. Although it's probably too late to get a reservation there. We'll make one for another night; you wouldn't want to miss it. We can go out to Old Massett to Sherri's Grill, which serves meals of locally caught fish and harvested vegetation."

"I guess we should eat something. Let's go out to Old Massett. I'd like to see more of the Haida village."

"Sounds good to me."

On the way out, Rob drove past the regional medical facility, which had a clinic, a hospital, and a personal care division.

"I love that they have a totem pole in front of it. It is so great that the Haida culture and art is being revitalized."

"Yes, tomorrow we should come back out to the gift shop. It's full of wonderful art, books, souvenir shirts, and so on. Deacon also told me that they're making a movie that is done completely in the Haida language. Because of the residence schools and missionaries, the Haida people lost their language, and only a handful of elders remember it. They're trying to bring it back, and they hope the film, *Edge of the Knife*, will promote it. I understand the younger kids are learning Haida in school now."

"That's great. These islands are so inspiring and peaceful. I can understand why artists and writers come to the islands to work on their projects. I could see myself living here for a few months each year. I understand that even in the winter the climate is usually more temperate here than on the prairies."

"Or the mountains in Colorado," Rob added. "I guess we've found something in common: love of Haida Gwaii."

By this time, they'd reached the restaurant, and soon they were enjoying a fish dinner. "These are the best fish and chips I've ever had," Penny declared. "It's so nice that it's made from fresh catch here off the islands."

"My salmon's great, too," Rob agreed.

Back at the cottage, they sat on the leather couch by the fireplace, drinking a cup of coffee. "It's not quite as good as Dr. Shirlee's, but it hits the spot," Rob commented.

"It's just fine," said Penny. "The evenings are still cool, so coffee by the fireplace is perfect. Thank you for putting up with me this evening and showing me around the island."

"My pleasure," Rob replied, smiling at her. Then he asked, "When's your flight back to the prairies?"

"I don't know. I haven't booked it yet. When Corbin sent me my plane ticket, it was one way. He thought I might want to make a holiday out of the trip so I could visit Libby and Sheryl. Oh, Libby. You don't have to keep me for the night. Libby said I was welcome at her place anytime."

"I'm sure normally you could, but it's getting late," Rob noted. "I'm sure they've put the kids to bed, and they may have retreated as well. I think Connor is on call tonight; he never knows when he might be called in the night because a baby might have decided to arrive. I'd hate to disturb their sleep."

"Good point," agreed Penny. "I think I'll get us another cookie," she added, pushing herself up from the couch with both hands. As she rose, a sudden noisy explosion exited her derriere.

Rob burst into laughter while Penny's face turned bright pink with embarrassment. "I'm so sorry and so embarrassed. I hate getting old and losing control."

Still chuckling, Rob said, "No problem, baby. Haven't I kept telling you you're so funny? Besides, it's a pleasure to hear the dumb speak."

Scowling at him but also grinning, Penny asked, "I suppose my bum is dumb like people who can't talk, because it doesn't usually make noise. Are you calling me 'baby' because I'm regressing to infancy?"

Pulling her back down onto the couch and putting his arm around her, Rob looked deep into her eyes and said, "No, of course not. I'm thinking it's just a sign that I'm liking you a lot, maybe even falling—"

Penny cut him off, saying, "Rob, we've only known one another a week!"

"So? At our age time moves quickly," he said, laughing. Leaning closer, he kissed her gently on her lips. Surprising both herself and Rob, Penny didn't pull away.

"Don't worry, Penny. I'm not going to force you into anything tonight. You can have the bedroom and I'll sleep on the couch. I do want to get to know you though, and I hope you'll stay on the islands for a while."

"Both Deacon and Sheryl have said you're a good guy, and they're right. I'd like to get to know you better, too. Right now, I guess we'd better get some sleep. I'm going to have to get back to their place early in the morning to get cleaned up."

"Actually, Deacon texted me and said Sheryl's put together a bag of your things. They'll bring it to town in the morning on their way to the shop so you can freshen up here."

"Oh, good. Sheryl was thinking farther ahead than I was. I guess I've been a little distracted." Penny smiled as she rose again from the couch. Leaning down, she gave him a quick kiss.

"Goodnight. See you in the morning," she said, moving into the bedroom and closing the door.

Stripping down to her underwear, Penny climbed into bed. Unable to get to sleep, her mind replayed everything that had happened in the past week with Rob. Could she love again? Would it work out or end in disaster like every other time had? Suddenly, she remembered the Ouija board nights with her friends in the dorm at Brandon University. When they'd asked who the love of her life would be, the planchette had moved from R to B. Had that stood for Rob Black? Leaving the answer to fate, she finally drifted off to sleep.

* * *

After getting her bag of fresh clothes and toiletries from Sheryl, Penny prepared herself for the day. Sheryl, of course, was curious as to how things had gone the night before. "Oh, fine," Penny had said, giving a vague response.

While the Crosses looked after their coffee shop, Rob and Penny went back out to Old Massett to tour the village and stop in at Sarah's Haida Arts and Jewellery Shop. Penny picked up several books about totem poles, Haida culture, and legends. Rob bought her an argillite killer whale pendant carved in the Haida style. When they left the store, he put the pendant chain around her neck. Locking it into place, he stroked the back of her neck and kissed it.

At the end of the day, Penny went with Sheryl and Deacon back to their lodge with plans to go with Rob out to Tow Hill and Agate Beach for the day. That evening, she and Sheryl sat on the lodge's porch with a glass of wine, reminiscing about the many times they had done the same thing at the Leighs' cabin on Jackfish Lake. Many serious topics had been covered back in those days, and suddenly their conversation took the same turn.

"What do you think is happening between you and Rob, Penny?" Sheryl asked.

"Good question, Sheryl. I'm not sure I have a definite answer. We've been enjoying one another's company as we explore the islands, but I'm not sure if it's leading anywhere. Of course, I'm skeptical about relationships because of my past experiences."

"I understand that, Penny, but I hope you can open yourself up to the possibility of love. Remember, you're never too old. You and Rob are both great people, and you both deserve a good relationship."

"Maybe. I guess even the close companionship of friendship is something folks our age need and look for."

"True," Sheryl agreed, "but I have a feeling your relationship has potential for more than that. Woman's intuition, I guess. Let's pack a nice picnic in the morning for your day out at Tow Hill."

"Thanks, Sheryl, for all you've done for me during my stay on the islands. I guess we should hit the hay; we need to get up early in the morning to make that picnic."

"Good idea," Sheryl said as she picked up their empty wine glasses to take inside. "Sweet dreams!" she added with a wink.

CHAPTER
TWENTY-FIVE

The next day, Penny and Rob drove through the tall cedar and spruce trees on the road to Tow Hill. They then walked through the scenic pathway to the back of Tow Hill. Along the way, they could see a large bare sand beach across the way because the tide was out. When they reached the back of the hill and walked on the rough lava rock to find the Blow Hole, Penny suddenly slipped on one of the wet rocks. Rob caught her before she fell and held her close, perhaps a little longer than necessary, but she stayed comfortably cuddled in his arms.

They finally found the Blow Hole, a hole within the lava rock that gushed water like a fountain when the tide came in. "I guess we aren't going to see the Blow," said Rob. "Maybe that's a good thing, as we'd probably get soaked. Let's go back to Agate Beach for our picnic. I'm getting a little hungry."

First, they walked along the rocky beach, looking for the green glass balls that floated in with the tide after falling from Japanese fishing nets. When they found a good spot, they spread a blanket and set up their lunch. Rob had also brought along a bottle of wine and some wine glasses, but they drank the Canada Dry ginger ale Penny had brought because their climbing and walking had made them hot and sweaty.

After they'd eaten, they sat on the beach and talked about their lives, especially about Rob's girls and grandchildren. Penny said, "You are so lucky to have a family. I know it must have been difficult to lose your wife, but you're so lucky to still have the results of your love."

In spite of the tears stinging her eyes and threatening to overflow, Penny revealed something she had only shared with Sheryl. "I lost a child once in a miscarriage." She gave no further details of the situation with Rodney.

"Oh, I'm so sorry, sweetheart," Rob said, wrapping his arm around her. "I'd be happy to share my grandkids with you. They need a nana with their papa."

"Well, Papa," Penny snorted, "we live too far apart for me to take on that role. And maybe they wouldn't want a Canuck grandma, eh?"

"That's fixable, eh." Rob laughed at his play on the Canadian expression.

"But you live in Florida, and I live in Manitoba. We're from two different countries and environments. How could that ever work?"

"Have you ever thought about getting out of that wicked prairie winter to spend some time in the south? We have a lot of Canadians in my active adult development. You have to watch your time there and get special travel health insurance, but it's doable. I'd certainly like to be in a cooler climate to avoid the heat and humidity of a Florida summer, so I wouldn't mind visiting Manitoba. I know lots of couples who go back and forth between countries. Since you have no ties left in your hometown, maybe you'd consider giving up your prairie place and we could buy a PMQ up here. Even better, maybe Deacon and Sheryl would consider selling their cottage to us. Since they're thinking about selling the coffee shop, they won't need to have a place to stay in town. Up here we could spend time with them, too, and maybe they'd visit us in Florida in the winter. What do you think?"

Rob had certainly given their situation a lot of thought, assuming they were going to be together. She needed to give that some thought, but it certainly wasn't out of the question. Before she could respond, Rob got a text from Deacon asking if they were at the cottage because they were ready to pick up Penny. Rob responded that they would be out on Agate Beach for a while still. He added that he'd take care of Penny.

"Looks like you're going to have another night at the cabin. Sheryl and Deacon are on their way home. I think that fate is playing in our favour. We have a lot to talk about, and this will give us more time now that we're in a serious discussion. It would be a shame to cut it off now."

"Good thing I left some toiletries at the cabin. Could we stop by Ladybird's Boutique on the way back to town so I can pick up a nightie and maybe something to wear tomorrow? My clothes are too dirty to wear again tomorrow."

"I can help you get out of them," Rob laughed. Then, more seriously, he added, "Sure, we can do that. Maybe we better start on our way back now."

When they got to the cottage, Penny showered and changed into her new nightie, covering it up with Rob's housecoat, which he'd left on the bed. Meanwhile, Rob had a sponge bath and changed his clothes, then put a frozen pizza in the oven and poured a couple of glasses of wine since they hadn't used any of the wine he'd brought for their picnic.

Walking into the kitchen, Penny observed Rob setting the table and pulling the pizza out of the oven to cut. He certainly looked comfortable in the kitchen. He seemed to be a home-body. Looking up at her, he smiled and said, "You do wonders to my tartan housecoat." Handing her a glass of wine, he added, "Come sit down. Supper isn't much, but it's ready."

"It smells delicious. It's just right after a busy day outdoors. Thank you for that, by the way. It was beautiful and fun."

They scarfed down the pizza and polished off a couple of glasses of wine. After cleaning up the kitchen, they considered sitting on the porch for a while. "I think I'm too tired," Penny said. Turning and moving toward the bedroom, she added, "I may go to bed soon."

"Sounds like a plan to me," Rob said. He came up behind her, wrapped his arms around her, and slid his hands inside the front of the robe, caressing her body over the silky nightgown. Penny sucked in her breath but didn't pull away. It had been a long time since she'd had such intimacy, and a shiver of pleasure ran through her.

Turning her around to face him, Rob said, "If it's all right with you, I've been thinking we should take the next step in our relationship."

"Are you afraid we might be too old?" Penny asked with a little giggle.

"I trust we don't have to worry about conception, do we? That's one advantage."

"No, Rob. That ship sailed a long time ago. You might have to put up with little unexpected explosions though."

"Oh, Penny, you are so funny. We are going to have a fun life together. We understand our limitations, but we'll work around them. I think we're both honest, sincere, and trustworthy. As Sheryl says, we're good people."

With that, he pulled her into his arms and kissed her deeply and passionately, to which she responded in kind. As he began moving them toward the bedroom, Penny suddenly said, "Stop. Wait a minute. I thought you said you were seeing someone in Florida. I won't let you abandon her."

"What I said, Penny, was that I'd gone out with a woman a couple of times and there might be potential, but that it was too early to know for sure. I really think she was more interested than I was, but that didn't stop her from dating others, too. Besides, as

your mother used to say, absence makes the heart grow fonder—
for somebody else." Laughing while drawing her in close again,
he continued, "And you're my somebody else."

Grinning, she wrapped her arms around his neck and drew
his face down for a kiss, then whispered, "And you are mine."

AUTHOR'S POSTSCRIPT
FOR THE READER

*A*s mentioned in the preface, some elements of the fictional town of Crocus Plains resemble those in my hometown of Killarney, Manitoba, but these elements have also been fictionalized. For example, when the new high school was built in Killarney, it was constructed on the outskirts of the west side of town, whereas the high school in Crocus Plains was built on the same grounds as the elementary school and the old stone high school.

Killarney also has a lovely lake and beach with a pavilion in the park, so I renamed the one in the novel Jackfish Lake. In googling the name, I discovered there is a Jackfish Lake in Saskatchewan and Alberta, but not Manitoba, so I thought it was a safe choice. I then discovered that there is a creek near Killarney called Jackfish Creek, but since the lake isn't called that, I stayed with the fictional name Jackfish Lake. Killarney had a movie theatre in town and a drive-in theatre south of town, so I named the fictional ones The Rainbow Theatre and Moonlight Drive-In. There were also Chinese restaurants in Killarney, so I named the fictional one in Crocus Plains Wing Ling's. I found there was such a restaurant in the Bronx, so I added "Wok" to it, making the one in the novel Wing Ling's Wok.

Some readers from Manitoba may recognize the name Crocus Plains as the name of a regional high school in Brandon,

Manitoba. I've always loved that name, and it seemed so appropriate for a town in Manitoba since the crocus is the provincial flower and plains are like prairies, so I adopted Crocus Plains for the name of my fictional small town.

Since readers from the Killarney area will likely connect with the fictional town, I avoided using any last names that were connected to Killarney in case readers thought the stories I told about fictional characters were the stories of real people. I researched and consulted relatives to check on names, so if any real names surface in the book, it was purely accidental. I, of course, had to keep the names Leigh, Campbell, Warren, and Jones because they were the last names of characters from Crocus Plains in the first novel. The main thing for readers to remember is that the novel and its characters are completely fictional.

I have been amazed over the years at how many people in the US and Canada are not aware of the International Peace Garden, so I wanted to include it in the book to make readers aware of its existence while also giving an explanation for how a Canadian girl like Sheryl might have ended up at the University of North Dakota. One thing that surprised me in my research was that it is called the Peace Garden singular; I grew up knowing it in the plural as the Peace Gardens, probably because of the many gardens visitors see while strolling up the central walkway. It has developed every decade, even obtaining remnants from one of the World Trade Center towers that were destroyed in the 9/11 attacks, which have been used to make a memorial.

In the postscript at the end of *Love on the Misty Isles*, I noted that there had been many changes during the years following the withdrawal of the military base from Haida Gwaii. A lot of entrepreneurial businesses developed, including hotels, bed-and-breakfasts, restaurants, stores, and even a real coffee shop. An artistic renaissance of the talented Haida creativity resulted in many shops being opened where the Haida people's work could be purchased, as well as the opening of personal art and carving studios that could be visited upon request. Their culture was also reaffirmed through museums, as well as carving sheds where totems are carved then raised on the islands to replace the ones lost to weathering or removal. Their language, which was lost due to missionaries and residential schools, is also being reborn.

Learning of all these changes in the forty years since we lived there in the mid-1970s while researching the setting for my debut novel, I wanted to return to the islands to see these changes for myself. My husband and I made that journey back in the summer of 2017. Details of this journey back to the Misty Isles can be read on my website's blog.

One of the pleasures of that trip was being able to meet and visit with Jack Litrell, the photographer who took the picture of Agate Beach and Tow Hill for the cover of my debut novel. He showed us his studio, which is filled with photos he had taken from around the world.

I was thrilled to meet and chat with Marlene Liddle, a clever, talented, and well-respected Haida woman who was my consultant and supporter while writing my first book. It was through Marlene that we first learned of the movie set on the islands to promote the use of the Haida language. She had been consulted on the costuming for the movie, and she showed us pictures of costumes she had made for it. *Edge of the Knife* was released in the summer of 2018, and it won awards at the Vancouver International Film Festival that fall. Marlene is a Haida cedar bark weaver who creates beautiful traditional and contemporary items and teaches others the art.

I am so glad we had the opportunity to revisit Haida Gwaii, the former Queen Charlotte Islands, to experience all these changes. I was able to draw on this experience to show the islands as they are in the more recent times when Penny visits them at the end of this sequel. I had mentioned in the first novel that a great website to see the islands' environment and villages is gohaidagwaii.ca For this novel, I have included a few real names of businesses. To see more of the current entrepreneurial work of people who love the islands and have created businesses to support their lives there, I recommend the website lovehaidagwaii.com. One example is a coffee shop that hadn't been there when we lived there, thus the reason I created the fictional Dr. Shirlee's Books 'n' Brew to play a central role in the connection of the characters. The real coffee shop is called The Ground Gallery and Coffee House. It supports the work of local artists as well as serving coffee and treats.

To explore more about places and things in this novel, I have included a list of websites and search terms for more in-depth information.

Many activities mentioned in this novel, such as hazing, male residents raiding women's dorm residences at a university, and little boys showing their interest in little girls by tackling them on the snow-covered school playgrounds would be unacceptable today. Back in the 1950s and 1960s, that's just the way it was. That doesn't make it right, but this novel represents the various times throughout the decades of the saga. I have also purposely included information demonstrating differences between the United States and Canada for the interest of readers from each country. I hope you've enjoyed this journey through time and Penny's life.

Websites and Facebook Pages of Interest

Websites:

gohaidagwaii.ca
lovehaidagwaii.com
haidaheritagecentre.com
haidagwaiimuseum.ca
canadianroyalpurplesociety.org
peacegarden.com
internationalmusiccamp.com

On Facebook:

Haida Cedar Bark Weaver - Traditional and
    Contemporary
Edge of the Knife
All About U Arts (a Haida art gallery and shop in
    Skidegate)

ONLINE SEARCH TERMS

Canadians in World War II or Canada's role in World War II
Canadians in Vietnam War or Canada and the Vietnam War

Rosemary Vaughn

Canadians and the liberation of the Netherlands
Canadian war brides
Manitoba prairie crocus images
Crocus Plains Regional Secondary School
    (Brandon, Manitoba)

ACKNOWLEDGEMENTS

I am so pleased that I was able to enlist Amy Sleper as my copyeditor. Amy had copyedited *Love on the Misty Isles*, so she was familiar with the connections between it and this sequel/prequel. We had a great working relationship, so I was grateful to be able to work with her again. Thank you, Amy, for your expertise and support.

Once again, I depended on my husband, Doug, as my medical consultant for health issues within this book. No hockey consultation was needed this time around. Thank you, sweetheart, for your professional help as well as for reading an early draft for input on growing up on the prairies. I also appreciated your taking over some household duties so that I could get this sequel completed. I also appreciate the support and pride of my daughter and son, who express their pride in their mother for exploring interests even at a mature age. My grandchildren think I'm a famous author and are anxious for me to write a children's chapter book for them.

I appreciate the assistance my sister Gwendolyn Dow and my cousin Sharon and her husband, Jack Folkett, gave me in avoiding use of real last names from the Killarney area. Jack also was able to clarify things in that area, like the existence of Jackfish Creek. I guess it takes one Jack to know another. My sister reminded me of the types of cars used during the eras in my book based on ones our father had, and she also clarified other items, such as where prairie crocuses grow.

Marilyn Lyons, who gave me wonderful support in the promotion of my debut book, was a helpful consultant on growing up on the prairies, particularly in the Killarney area, as we were childhood friends and classmates.

I am also appreciative of assistance from friends who attended Brandon University with me in clarifying or confirming programs, activities, events, and rules. Thank you, Eric and Simonne Dickie, Margie Lisowski, and Bunny Williamson.

I am grateful to my niece Terri Hall for sharing photographs of prairie grain fields that gave me inspiration for my vision of a book cover for this novel *Penny for Your Thoughts*.

I cannot thank my neighbor and friend Catherine Larson enough for her tech expertise and her willingness to assist me when I had a problem at a moment's notice.

I am, of course, indebted to the readers of my award-winning debut novel, *Love on the Misty Isles*, for their urging my writing of a sequel. It was their encouragement that inspired me to write this sequel/prequel. Thank you, readers, for your support.

Author Biography

orn and raised on the Canadian prairies, Rosemary Vaughn immigrated with her family to the northern plains of the United States in the mid-1970s. Her creative imagination was evident early in elementary school when the numbers in addition columns became characters about whom she imagined stories as she did her sums. A high school English teacher and then professor of teacher education, Rosemary had previously published works focused on academics. She, however, continued to feed her creative impulses by writing skits and puppet plays for church and community use, as well as personal poetry and essays.

Now retired, she has resumed her interest in creative writing, and she enjoys composing humorous essays on everyday life. Her award-winning debut novel, *Love on the Misty Isles*, was her first foray into fiction. From her summer lake cabin in Minnesota and her winter retreat in Florida, Rosemary continues to develop her interest and hone her skills in creative writing, thus adopting the title Pine to Palm Writer. Responding to requests from her readers, she wrote this sequel/prequel to *Love on the Misty Isles*. She hopes you enjoy this family saga focusing on Penny; therefore, she is giving you a Penny for your thoughts.

Follow Rosemary on her website at www.rosemaryvaughn. com or her Facebook author page at www.facebook.com/ authorrosemaryvaughn.